THE BATTLE OF
LOOKOUT
MOUNTAIN

Bonnets and Bugles Series · 7

THE BATTLE OF LOOKOUT MOUNTAIN

GILBERT MORRIS

MOODY PRESS
CHICAGO

ISBN: 0-8024-0917-2

3 5 7 9 10 8 6 4

Printed in the United States of America

To Troy and Jason Freeman—
Two straight arrows
I hope you like this story!

Contents

1
Home Again

As soon as Leah Carter dumped the bucket of field corn into the trough, all seven suckling pigs came running across the lot. She smiled at their squeals, and as their pink snouts pushed into the corn she laughed at their eagerness.

"You have the worst manners of any pigs I ever saw! Look at you, Jacob—shoving your brother out of the way! Now you stop that!"

Leah had named all of the pigs after characters in the Bible, and now she saw that she had named them well. The one named Cain was snapping at the one she had named Abel. She caught Cain's tail and dragged him backward.

"You give your brother a fair share of that corn!" she scolded.

But Cain was true to his name. He snorted and bit at her wickedly, and when she released him he plunged back into the mass of squirming piggish bodies.

Leah gave up on the pigs and leaned on the fence to watch as they chewed and grunted. "You look like some of the Franklin family at the church picnic. I never saw such greed!" she said aloud.

But there was a smile on her face for she loved animals and took pleasure in raising them. Somewhere down the line she knew they would all either be sold or end up on her plate as pork chops.

However, she had learned to forget this—or at least put it out of her mind.

A slight July breeze blew Leah's hair and cooled her face. She was a tall girl of fifteen and saw herself as gawky. Her mother had said, "You're going to be *stately*, Leah, not a giantess!" and another time Ma had said sharply, "Stop stooping over! God gave you a tall, good figure—now don't be ashamed of being tall."

Leah, like many young girls her age, was too conscious of her appearance. Actually she had nothing to be ashamed of. She had light blonde hair, very fine, that hung to her waist when it was not braided and coiled around the back of her head as it was now. Her eyes were a light green that sometimes seemed almost blue. One of her uncles, who had been to the ocean, said, "Leah, your eyes are just the color as the sea at certain times of the morning—not quite blue, not quite green, just a little bit of each."

She had an oval face with a shapely wide mouth, and her complexion was fair. She had a few freckles across her nose—which she hated.

Leah drifted off in thought, wondering how Jeff Majors would think of the way she was growing up. Jeff was one year older. They had birthdays on the same date, June 15, and until the time that the Majorses left Kentucky, they had spent every birthday party together.

The thought of Jeff's leaving saddened Leah. "I hate this old war," she muttered. Her brother, Royal, had gone to fight for the Union, while Jeff's family had gone to Virginia to side with the South. Now Jeff was a drummer boy in the Confederate army—his father was a major—and, strangely enough, Jeff's older brother, Tom, was back here with the Carters after having had his leg shattered at Gettysburg.

For a while Leah thought of the days when she and Jeff had roamed the hills hunting birds' eggs and chasing possums and raccoons, or fishing. "I wish the war was all over," she said, "and everything could be like it was again. I wish—"

Suddenly strong arms wrapped around Leah, pinning her arms to her side and squeezing her so that she could not get her breath. She was lifted clear off the ground, and she squealed in sudden fear. The arms merely tightened, and she felt a face press against the back of her head—and then she got a resounding kiss on her right cheek!

"Is that you all got to do—stay out here and watch pigs, Leah?"

Leah felt herself released, and she whirled to see Royal standing before her, grinning.

"Royal!" She threw her arms around him and pressed her face against his chest, and his arms closed around her again. Fear that he would be hurt or even killed in battle had been with Leah every day her brother had been gone. And now he was back!

Trying to put an angry expression on her face, she said, "Royal, I could shoot you! Why didn't you tell us you were coming home?"

"Didn't know it," he said airily.

Her brother was not tall—not over five eight or nine—but he was strongly built. He had a cheerful face, hair only a little darker than Leah's, and amazingly light blue eyes. They looked like cornflowers, Leah once told him. He was called "the Professor"

11

by the soldiers in his unit, for he had spent one year in college and usually had his nose in a book.

He reached out and pinched Leah's chin. "Anyway, I wanted to surprise you," he said.

"Have you been to the house to see Ma and Pa?"

"No, just got here. Come on—you can take me in."

Leah grabbed Royal's hand as they walked toward the house. She fired questions at him, which he answered as best he could. They climbed the steps to the white two-story farm home, entered through the front door, and went down the wide hall that led to the kitchen.

"Ma—Pa—look who's here."

Dan and Mary Carter rushed to Royal and embraced him.

"Why, Son, what a great surprise!" Mr. Carter said. "How long can you stay?"

His father was thin, with the sickly look of the chronically ill. He had brown hair, faded blue eyes, and a firm mouth under a scraggly mustache. He had been shot up badly in the Mexican War and now was a sutler. He followed the Union army in his wagon, carrying supplies such as paper, pins, needles and thread, and special foods that the soldiers liked. Leah sometimes went with him.

"How long can I stay?" Royal repeated. "Long enough to eat you out of house and home, Pa." He hugged his mother with one arm and shook his father's hand at the same time. "Ma, I'm expecting to be fed like the Thanksgiving turkey before he becomes the dinner!"

Mrs. Carter was an attractive woman. She had the same blonde hair and blue-green eyes as his sister Leah, and there was a strength in her that everyone recognized. "I might know you'd come home hungry," she said. "You sit right down there. I'll start making one of those cherry pies."

"Make one just for me, Ma."

"You start the pie, Ma," Leah said. "Come, Royal—I've got a surprise for you."

Their parents looked at her as if they knew what was on her mind. "You bring him back soon," Mrs. Carter said.

"Where are we going?" Royal asked as Leah hauled him by the hand out of the kitchen and through the back door.

"You'll see." She pulled him down the steps and then turned him to face the huge walnut tree that shaded the backyard. Underneath it a small group sat on a quilt spread on the ground—Royal's other sisters, Sarah and Morena, and a man playing with a year-old blonde baby.

At the sight of the man, Royal dropped Leah's hand and yelled, "Tom—Tom Majors!" and ran across the yard.

Tom Majors looked up. Tom had been Royal's best friend since boyhood. He was wearing a checked red-and-white shirt and gray trousers.

Royal crossed the yard in bounds, dropped down beside his friend, and beat him on the shoulders. "Tom, you old son of a gun, what are you doing here?"

The last he had heard, Tom was a sergeant in the Confederate army, and Royal couldn't imagine how he had gotten back to neutral ground in Kentucky—right here at his own home.

Suddenly a cry rose from Tom's lips, and Royal stopped abruptly and drew back. Tom Majors was dark complexioned, but now his face was pale, and there was pain in his eyes.

"What's wrong, Tom? I didn't hurt you, did I?" But even as Royal spoke, he saw that Tom's left leg was missing below the knee. He stood up quickly. "Well—say—I'm sorry—I didn't know, Tom."

Tom Majors pulled himself to his feet. Reaching out, he took the pair of crutches that was leaning against the tree trunk and settled them under his arms. "That's all right, Royal," he said quietly.

Silence fell over the group then. The girl beside him—Royal's sister Sarah—was the first to recover. "I'm so glad to see you, Royal," and as he put his arms around her, she kissed him on the cheek. "How long can you stay?"

"Maybe a couple of weeks," Royal said. He was still stunned by Tom's injury, and his mind swirled as he tried to think of what to say. Finally, being an honest young man, he turned to his friend and asked, "Where did you get hit, Tom? Gettysburg?"

"That's right."

Royal waited for him to say more, but Tom Majors simply pressed his lips tightly together.

"Well, I'm glad it wasn't worse," Royal said quickly. "How did you get here?"

"Jeff and Sarah brought me. I was hurt too bad to travel back to Virginia. She'll tell you about it. I'll be seeing you around, Royal." Tom put out the crutches and swung his body along, his face hidden. He disappeared around the house, and Royal stared after him.

Then Royal felt a hand and looked down to see his eleven-year-old sister Morena tugging at him. She too had blonde hair, but there was a blankness in her blue eyes. She had developed into a beautiful

14

child physically, but mentally she never had matured.

Royal swept her up in his arms. "Morena," he said, "you are getting prettier all the time."

She laughed and patted his cheek.

Sarah and Leah stood quietly waiting as he played with the child.

And then he looked up. "Tell me about it."

Sarah said quietly, "It was a miracle really, Royal. I'd gone to Gettysburg to be with Abigail Munson. She was having her first child and was pretty much alone. I was there when the battle took place. Tom and Jeff were there with the army. When Tom lost his leg and couldn't travel, we had to do something. It was impossible to get back to Virginia. Both he and Jeff would have been captured." Her blue eyes were thoughtful as she remembered that time. "I bought a wagon and team—we traveled at night, dodging Union patrols until we got back here."

"Tom's changed, Royal," Leah said. "His leg is healing, but he seems to have given up. He just won't take an interest in anything—he's not the Tom we knew."

Royal glanced in the direction where Tom had disappeared. "Maybe I can help him," he said. "We were always real close."

Sarah hesitated. "I hope you can."

The thought came to Royal that Sarah was closer to Tom than anyone else—they had been almost engaged before the war started. He studied her face and knew that, if Sarah could not help Tom, it would be difficult for anyone to help.

"Well, I'll do the best I can—we all will," he said. Then he knelt beside the baby on the quilt. "Look at

Esther—she's growing like a tadpole turning into a frog."

"That's awful, Royal!" Sarah protested. "To call a child a frog! She's the prettiest baby that ever was!"

Esther was the only sister of Tom and Jeff. Her mother had died giving birth to her, and since all the Majors men were in the Confederate army, the Carters, their old neighbors, had taken the child to raise.

Royal picked her up, and she squealed. He said, "She *is* good-looking, the best-looking female on the place." He winked at his sisters. "But don't tell Ma I said so."

At supper that night there was great rejoicing. Mrs. Carter loaded the table, with help from her two daughters: pork chops, fresh ham, fried chicken, mashed potatoes, candied yams, green beans— and two luscious cherry pies in crumbly crusts.

Royal finally leaned back after his third piece of pie. "It would be a sin to eat any more of this," he declared.

"It was a sin about a half hour ago, I think, Son." His father grinned at him. "I believe we have all committed gluttony tonight."

"Tell us some more about the army, Royal," Leah said eagerly.

"Well, Tom here could tell you more than I could. For us it's been either bored to death or scared to death."

Sarah was sitting next to Tom. "What do you mean?" she asked.

Royal had noticed that Tom had scarcely touched his food. He'd been mostly just pushing it around with his fork. He had not said ten words

16

either. But at mention of the war, his hand closed tightly on his fork, the knuckles growing white.

"I mean it's either weeks or even months of drilling—the same old thing every day. Then you go into a battle, and for about one day or two you're scared to death. Is that the way it was with you fellas, Tom?"

"Just about." Tom's face was pale, and his voice was low. He did not contribute anything else to the conversation although he had been through every major battle.

Since Tom had been on the opposite side, from time to time Royal had had nightmares that one day on the battlefield he would face a young fellow in a gray uniform and that fellow would be his best friend, Tom Majors.

Leah obviously saw that Tom was not going to participate in the conversation. "Come on into the parlor, Royal," she said. "I want to show you some pictures. A traveling photographer came, and we all had our pictures made."

"But I haven't had my coffee yet."

"I'll bring it to you," his mother said. "You go on in. You girls too. I'll do the dishes."

The girls protested, but not very much. Sarah finally said, "You come too, Ma. We can all wash the dishes later."

The parlor was a pleasant room with whale oil lamps on the heavy walnut tables. Royal and his sisters seated themselves on the horsehide sofa, Royal in the middle with Leah and Sarah on each side. Morena came to sit on his lap, and across the room Tom sat, holding the baby, Esther. He stroked her hair gently and, as the others exclaimed and laughed over the pictures, he seemed to be far away.

Perhaps he was thinking about his father, now a major in the Confederate army, and his brother, Jeff, a private—wondering if they were about to go into another battle. He glanced down at his pinned-up left trouser leg, and a spasm of pain crossed his face.

From across the room Royal saw it, and his heart constricted. He said nothing, but it hurt him to see Tom Majors, who had always been the most cheerful young man at any party, just sitting there, cut off from all the rest of them.

Finally the women went back to the kitchen to do the dishes, and Mr. Carter yawned and said, "I've had a long day—I'm going to bed. It's good to have you home, Royal," he said, and then he left.

Royal sat on the sofa with Morena beside him. She was content to hold his hand and stroke it lovingly. He smiled down at her. The only language she really understood was the expression on someone's face or the tone of voice.

"You're mighty pretty, Morena," he murmured. Then he looked across at Tom and Esther. "She sure is a beauty, Esther is."

"Yes, she is. She looks like Ma," Tom said. He smoothed the blonde hair and touched the silky cheek with his finger. Esther grabbed it and pulled at it vigorously. This brought a smile to Tom's face, the first of the evening.

For a while the two men talked, but it was an effort. No matter how much Royal spoke, Tom answered only in monosyllables. At last Tom rose, put the baby on the floor, and said, "I guess I'll go to bed too. It's good to have you back, Royal."

Royal sat beside Morena, listening to the thump of Tom's crutches echo from the hall. Then he heard a door slam. Finally he picked up Esther, and he and Morena went into the kitchen, where his mother dried her hands and carried the baby off to bed.

When it was past everyone's bedtime, Royal was left for a few moments alone with Sarah.

"It's real bad, Sarah," Royal said quietly. "Is he always like this?"

"I haven't seen him smile hardly twice since he got here," Sarah answered slowly.

"But surely he knows that life's not over!"

"He acts as though it is. He never talks about what is going to happen. He doesn't talk about anything."

"But there are ways that he can be helped. There are artificial legs. He could get one of those."

Sarah turned and faced her brother. "Ezra has tried to talk him into that."

Ezra Payne, Royal thought. Their hired hand, who was very clever with tools. Although young, he could make almost anything out of wood.

"Ezra could make one too. But Tom won't listen."

"But we've got to convince him."

"You remember Gus Springer?"

"Sure, I remember Gus." A light came into Royal's eyes, and he said, "Why, yes—*he's* got an artificial leg, and he gets around great."

"Yes, he does—and I asked him to come out and talk to Tom, and he did."

"Well, how did it go? You know Gus. He can do almost anything—you hardly know he's lost a leg. But—" Seeing the look on his sister's face, Royal asked quietly, "He wouldn't listen to Gus?"

"No, and he got angry with me for asking him here." Sarah's eyes filled with tears, and she abruptly dashed them away. "I—I don't know what we are going to do about Tom."

A feeling of helplessness filled Royal Carter. He put his hands on Sarah's shoulders. "We'll do something," he said firmly. "God saved Tom's life. He's not through with him yet!"

2
A New Face

Come on, Tom, you don't have to dance, but you always liked music. I don't think you ought to sit here at home."

Royal had found Tom on the parlor sofa, watching Esther crawl around on the floor.

"I don't think so, Royal," he said.

A frown passed across Royal's face. He had promised Sarah and Leah that he would do his best to get Tom to go to the dance that was being held at the schoolhouse. They had both warned him that it would be useless to try, for Tom had not left the house more than once or twice since he had come back to Pineville.

Biting his lip, Royal tried once again. "Look, Tom, maybe you feel out of place, your being Confederate and all, but that's all over now."

Tom's eyes flashed. "I may be a cripple," he snapped, "but I'm still a Confederate! People around here aren't going to forget that. Leave me alone, will you, Royal! If you want to help me, *that's* what you can do—just leave me alone."

Royal wanted to argue, but he saw from the stubborn look on Tom's face that arguing would be useless. He turned and left the room and found Sarah and Leah ready to go. They had obviously been listening to his conversation with Tom.

Sarah shook her head warningly. "It won't work, Royal," she said in a whisper.

They went outside, and Royal helped Sarah and Leah into the carriage. He climbed in then and spoke to the horses, and the buggy was soon bumping along the road headed for the schoolhouse. They said little, everyone avoiding the subject of Tom Majors. However, Royal knew that Tom was on their minds.

Royal did say, "He'll come around. It'll just take a little time." He saw that Sarah was unhappy, but he knew her well enough to say no more on the subject.

They pulled up at the schoolhouse. The yard was already full of buggies, wagons, and saddle horses. The sound of music was wafted on the warm summer air, and as Royal helped the girls down, he said, "This is a little bit different from what I've been used to lately."

Sarah reached over and straightened his collar. He was wearing his uniform and looked rather dashing in it. Although not strikingly handsome, Royal was nonetheless attractive. His blue eyes sparkled, and he looked trim and fit.

Lanterns hung over the outside platform that had been built for the dancers, and he looked around at the crowd. "I guess all the pretty girls have been taken since I left for the army."

"No, there are lots of them without their young men." Leah smiled at him. "You better take a stick, Royal, to beat them off!"

He laughed at her and pinched her cheek. "None of them will be as pretty as you, Sis," he said, "except maybe for Sarah here. But you both look like angels."

Sarah wore a rose-colored dress, and her hair was done up in a way that he had not seen before.

She was a beautiful girl, and at once she was claimed by a young man who took her off to dance.

Leah was claimed by one of her youthful friends, David Peterson, who lived just down the road. He was overweight, and his collar was so tight his face seemed to be swollen. He was hopelessly in love with Leah, who liked him but was not nearly as much taken with him as he was with her.

As the sisters had said, Royal became the center of attention almost instantly. He found himself dancing with Maude Kimberly, a short, plump girl of seventeen, who batted her eyelashes at him in a way she evidently thought was very fetching. She was wearing a bright red dress that emphasized her plumpness. She looked in fact rather like an over-ripe tomato, although Royal, of course, did not say so.

After that dance, he danced with Mable Conroy, an old friend, and then he sought out the refreshment table, where he was surrounded by the men. They asked him eagerly about his war experiences. He spoke about them briefly, and then Sarah pulled him away.

"You can talk to the men down at the feed store tomorrow. That's where they go to chew tobacco and spit and decide how to run the country," she said with a mischievous glint in her eye. "Tonight you just have fun!"

Even as she spoke, a clear tenor voice rose up, and Royal looked around to find the singer.

"Why, that's Drake Bedford," he said. He listened for a moment. "Drake always was the best singer—and one of the best fiddle players."

"Oh, yes, he's in his element at these dances." Sarah hesitated. "But he's kind of wild, Royal."

"Yes, he always was. All the time drinking and fighting with some other fellow over some girl. He still doing that?"

"I'm afraid so. He is handsome though, isn't he?"

Royal examined the features of the young singer. He was tall, over six feet, strong-looking and athletic. He had crisp brown hair, gray eyes, and was wearing a stylish gray suit with a black string tie. When he finished his song, the musicians struck up, and he grabbed a young lady standing nearby and began swinging her around the platform.

"How about a dance with you, Sis?" Royal asked.

"You didn't come to dance with your *sister*, Royal!" Sarah protested.

"Well, let's see who I can dance with. There's Amy Perkins. She always walks all over your feet—don't want her. And there's Roseanne Grangerford—she wants to talk about poetry all the time—and bad poetry too. She doesn't know the difference between good and bad." His eyes ran over the crowd, and he halted his cataloging of the young ladies abruptly. "Who's *that*, Sarah?"

Sarah looked in the direction of Royal's glance. "Oh, that's Lorraine Jenkins."

"Who is she? She's new around here, isn't she?"

"She's Hamilton Jenkins's niece. You know him and his wife, Mae, don't you?"

"Yes, but I didn't think anybody as homely as that pair could have any relatives as pretty as she is."

"You shouldn't say that! The Jenkinses are fine people!"

"Yes, they are. I was just kidding!"

Royal watched the girl Lorraine Jenkins. She was with a man he did not know, and the man was obviously taken with her. She was a small girl, and the lantern light glinted on her auburn hair, making it look almost red. She had an oval face, and there was something vivacious about her. He could tell from her chin and the side of her face that she was strong-willed—and that she had lovely eyes and full red lips.

"I suppose I ought to take pity on her and pull her away from that clodhopper that is probably walking all over her feet."

"You always were chivalrous, Royal," Sarah teased.

Royal made his way toward the couple and tapped the man on the shoulder. "Mind if I cut in?"

"Well—"

Royal did not wait for him to finish but took the girl's hand and swung her away, leaving her partner looking rather disconsolate and half angry.

"My name is Royal Carter," he said. "I don't believe we've met."

"No, I'm Lorraine Jenkins."

"Happy to know you, Miss Jenkins. You're new in town here, are you?"

"Yes, my home is in Chattanooga. I'm here on a visit to my uncle and aunt."

"Oh, yes, Mr. and Mrs. Jenkins—they're fine people. Are you enjoying your visit?"

From across the platform Leah watched as the pair danced. She was suddenly interrupted by a voice that said, "Well, now, it's Miss Leah, ain't it?"

She looked around to see a tall, gangly young man standing behind her. She knew him at once, for he was almost unforgettable. He had tow-colored hair, parted in the center, light blue eyes, and

25

craggy features. He looked a little like a very young Abraham Lincoln with his homely expression.

"Yes, it's Mr. Rose, isn't it?"

"Well—" the young man grinned "—that's what the preacher calls me. A. B. Rose is my name, but folks just call me Rosie. I think I might be able to make it through at least one dance if you'd like, Miss Leah."

"Why, of course, Rosie."

He had huge feet, but he didn't tread on her toes. As they stepped onto the platform, he cleared his throat. "Don't reckon I'm long for this world, Miss Leah."

Looking up, Leah was amazed. "Why, what's the matter, Rosie?"

"I'm not a well man," he said solemnly. There was a gloomy look on his face. "I'm lucky that I've lived to be as old as I have, but it can't go on forever."

Actually he seemed to be a rather strong young man, she thought, despite his gangly frame. His hands were corded with muscles, and there was a healthy glow to his face.

Still, he began to catalog his physical ailments. "My rheumatism is doing better, but that's because I got that medicine out of Memphis for it. But I got these terrible shooting pains in my legs. They can't be growing pains—at least, I hope they ain't. Probably some dreadful disease that ain't been discovered yet."

Soon Leah began to suspect that Rosie's ailments were all imaginary. He led her over to the refreshment center and ate three pieces of pie so quickly that it was almost magical. Leah's eyes twinkled. "Do you suppose pie is good for your ailments, Rosie?"

"There's no telling," he said, his voice almost funereal. He reached for another piece. "Man that's born of this world is of few days—that's what the Scripture says."

Leah looked across the platform. "You and Drake are great friends, aren't you?"

"Oh, that we are, Miss Leah. He's been mighty good to me and my misfortune."

Leah then remembered hearing that this very young man, who claimed to be an invalid, had been jailed along with Drake Bedford for fighting. The two of them had taken on five toughs from over in North Pine Community and had thrashed them soundly. Now she was sure that Rosie was indeed self-diseased.

The music struck up again, and Rosie sighed heavily. "Well—" he shoved a bite of pie into his mouth "—I guess we better see if I can hold up one more time around that floor."

As Rosie led her to the platform again, Leah said, "Look, my brother's with that new girl in town."

"Oh, that Miss Lori Jenkins?"

"That's her. See—that's my brother, Royal. Remember him?"

"Sure do, but I wish he wouldn't force himself on Miss Lori."

"Why, I don't think he'd do that!" Leah was puzzled. "Why do you say that, Rosie?"

"Well, Drake—he fancies himself first where the ladies are concerned. And he's got his head set on impressing her. I never saw him so set on courting a gal."

Royal had been enjoying his dance with Lorraine Jenkins. He had gotten things to the point where she had asked him to call her Lori, and he was working up to requesting permission to call on her. At that moment a hand clapped him on the shoulder harder than was necessary. He turned to see Drake Bedford grinning at him.

"Hello, Royal. I'm taking your girl away!"

"Why, sure, Drake." Royal stepped back as was the custom. "I'll see you later, Miss Lori."

"Not if I can help it!" Drake Bedford said.

Drake swept Lori away, and when they were out on the floor again he said, "Now, you don't want to get too interested in that young man."

Lori smiled at him. She had never seen a man with more self-confidence. *A little bit too much sometimes,* she thought. "He looks fine in his uniform, doesn't he? My uncle says he's been in some of the battles."

"Oh, sure, that's the way these soldiers are. Throw on a uniform and hear a gun go off—then to hear them tell it, they won the whole war. I see them all the time like that."

Something about this response displeased Lori. "I don't think Royal is like that. He seems a rather modest young man."

Drake looked down at her. He seemed very tall and strong, and his grasp on her hand tightened. "You can't use but one fellow courting at a time, and I reckon that I'm that fellow."

Royal was enjoying the evening thoroughly. It had been a long time since he'd been home, and he was glad to see his old friends again. He received numerous offers to come and take supper—mostly from mothers with marriageable daughters. But he managed to fend most of them off.

Then it was the last dance, and he managed to get close to Lori again. She turned to him with a smile.

"I don't have much time, Miss Lori," he said. "Ordinarily I'd wait two or three weeks to come calling, but I'm asking now."

Lori hesitated. "Well, of course!" she said. "Why don't you come to supper tomorrow night? At half past five?"

"Will that be all right with your uncle and aunt?"

"Oh, yes, they'll be glad to have you. They are always very supportive of young men in the army."

Then they heard a muffled shout, and people began leaving the platform.

"What's going on?" Royal asked.

"I don't know. Let's go see."

They followed the crowd, and Royal soon saw that a fight was in progress. "Why, that's Drake!" he exclaimed.

"Yes, it is."

There was such an odd quality in Lori's voice that Royal gave her a questioning look.

"That's Darrell Hopkins he's fighting with," she said.

All at once Royal understood. "I see. Over you, I suppose?"

"Oh, it's so silly. Darrell is just a good friend, but Drake's decided that he's my keeper." A sudden thought seemed to come to her, and she asked, "Are you good friends with Drake?"

"Not particularly."

"Then I'm afraid he'll make trouble for you if you come calling."

Royal smiled down at her. She looked very fetching in her light blue party dress. Her cheeks were flushed, and her eyes were large and beautifully shaped. They were shaded by the heaviest lashes he had ever seen, and she had skin like cream.

"Well, Drake will just have to do what he has to do—but I'll be there for supper tomorrow night, Miss Lori."

"Good!" she said. "I'll try to talk to Drake so that he doesn't start any foolishness."

"I sure have enjoyed dancing with you, Miss Leah," Rosie said. "Surprised I made it, but you must be good medicine for a sick man."

"It looks like that fellow Drake was fighting was hurt pretty bad," Leah said, a worried expression on her face.

"Oh, he probably got a few bones broke and maybe his nose smooshed, but that's how Drake is. I don't guess Darrell will be courting anybody for a while." Rosie hesitated, then said, "You might tip your brother off. I see he's been with Miss Lori a lot. Tell him it might be better for his health if he didn't do that."

"He can see anyone he wants to!"

"Well, of course he can. It's a free country." Rosie shrugged and then apparently put the matter from his mind. "Look. I got these pills out of Cincinnati last week. They're supposed to be good for indigestion. Do they look all right to you?"

3

"Just Leave Me Alone"

Sarah said very little the day following the dance; otherwise she went about her work as usual. Late that afternoon, while she and her mother were making a quilt, the subject of Tom Majors came up.

"Sarah," her mother said quietly, "you're troubled about Tom."

"Yes, I am. Aren't you?"

Mrs. Carter's fingers flew, putting tiny stitches in the bed cover. The colorful top displayed little Dutch boys and girls with odd hats, made from scraps from other sewing projects. "Yes, of course I am!" she said.

Sarah looked up, her dark blue eyes distressed. "I don't know what he's going to do. I don't think he does either. It's just like all the strength has been drained out of him. All the purpose. He was always so excited about everything, Tom was. Now it's almost like he's—like he's dead inside."

Mrs. Carter took another stitch. "You wouldn't agree to marry Tom before because he was going to be in the Confederate army . . ."

"I know!" Sarah thought for a moment and then said, "But now he won't be in the army."

"Maybe not, but he's still sympathetic to the South. I'm not sure such a marriage would work."

This was exactly what Sarah had feared. She clamped her lips together, and for some time the two women said nothing. The loudest sound in the room was the buzzing of a fly that zigzagged around Sarah's head. It lit on her cheek, and she brushed it away angrily. "I don't see why life has to be like this!" she said rebelliously.

Sarah was known as a calm, gentle girl, rarely showing anger, always ready to take the way of peace. But the war had ground on for more than two years. Many of the young men in this part of the country had died and were buried on battlefields with outlandish names. Her own brother lay heavily on her heart, and she dreaded for him to go back and face the fire of battle. Now she threw her needle down and got up, saying, "Sometimes I think it's unfair!"

Her mother looked up at her. "You don't think *God's* unfair, do you?"

"Oh, no, I don't mean that! It's just that . . . well . . . I don't know what I mean!" She knew she was close to tears, and she left the room hurriedly, leaving her mother looking disturbed.

Later that morning Tom brought Esther, wearing only a diaper, out into the yard. He wanted to keep her out of the sun, and they lolled under the spreading walnut tree. Looking at the baby, he remembered his mother, and it was with a pang that he saw how much Esther was like her. Memories flowed through Tom's mind—he did not think of the future. In his mind, his life had ended when the shell shattered his leg at Gettysburg.

A cheery call came from the road, and Tom looked up to see Pete Mangus slide off the blue-nosed mule he called Clementine. Pete talked to her constantly as he rode the hills of Kentucky delivering the United States mail.

"Now, you wait here, Clementine. I'll be right back."

Pete was a small man with sandy hair and blue eyes. He did not have a tooth in his head and refused to get false teeth. He somehow managed without teeth—could even eat steak, "gumming," he said. But being toothless made his speech a little difficult to understand. His cheeks were sunken in, and his chin almost met his nose where his face was collapsed.

But he was a cheerful fellow. "Hi, Tom. Letter for you."

Tom tucked his maimed leg back under the other in an automatic gesture, as if to hide the injury. He took the letter and said, "Thanks, Pete. I think there's some lemonade in the house. No ice, but it's wet."

"That sounds good!"

Pete watched Tom unfold the letter. He might not have teeth, but he had a tremendous curiosity, and now he waited to get a report on what was inside the letter. His bright blue eyes were sharp, and as Tom read he inquired, "Good news, I hope?"

The letter was neither good nor bad. Looking up at the mailman, Tom shrugged. "A letter from my father."

"Oh, in Virginia! What's he say the Confederate army is going to do? Is Bob Lee going to come out and fight again?"

Tom could not help smiling at the man's curiosity. "Well, I don't think General Lee gives my father all his plans, Pete." He felt the eyes of the mailman on him as he finished reading and put the letter back in the envelope. "Not much news," he reported, managing a smile. "Sorry not to have more gossip for you."

Pete drew his thin shoulders together. "Well, I don't care!" he said and stomped off toward the house. He knocked on the door, and Leah met him.

"I bet you've come for some lemonade, Pete!"

"Well, now," Pete mumbled, grinning toothlessly, "I reckon that would go down pretty easy."

Pete Mangus sat on a stool watching Leah peel potatoes. He gossiped about the neighbors up the road and down the road. Knowing everyone in the county, he kept up with all the local news.

"And how's that young fellow you're so interested in—Jeff Majors?" he asked.

Leah was accustomed to Pete's ways. "He's fine, Pete. Back in Virginia now."

"I'll bet he's right jealous of that young Ezra working around here. Which one of them do you like the best?"

"I like them both, Pete. Would you like some more lemonade?"

The mailman nodded and noisily guzzled down another glassful. Then he said, "What about Sarah? Is she fixing to marry young Tom out there? Even if he ain't got no foot?"

Leah gently answered, "I suppose that's their business. They don't tell me everything. Well, I've got to go to work," she said, hinting strongly that it was time for Pete to leave.

He finished his lemonade and walked out to the yard, where Tom was tossing a small ball toward a chortling Esther. "Got to go on my way, Tom. Be back to see you in three or four days."

"So long, Pete."

As Pete Mangus mounted Clementine and went plodding on, raising clouds of dust, Tom thought of the letter he had received. The lack of hope in the letter surprised him. His father had always been opposed to the war on general principles. But he believed that states had a right to choose their own government, even though he was not a slaveholder himself. Now, however, Tom could tell by the tone of the letter that Pa had pretty well resigned himself to the fact that the South could not win.

Somehow this did not surprise Tom. He himself had come to this conclusion some time ago; and now that he knew he would no longer be in action, the war and secession seemed even further distant.

A door slammed, and he looked up to see Sarah coming.

She had brought a fresh diaper, and she smiled down at Esther. "I think she needs changing!" Despite the baby's protests, she held her down and carried out the job. "There. Now you're all dry again!"

"I could do that!" Tom said.

"Well, I know," Sarah said quickly. "But I just like babies so much. It's been so nice to have one to fuss over!" She sat down across from him and watched Esther crawl about in the grass. "I hope she doesn't eat a bug or a worm or something!"

"I don't guess it would hurt her," Tom remarked. Sarah was looking very pretty, he thought. She had on a yellow dress that was particularly attractive. It had small white flowers embroidered on it, and he knew she had made it herself. Her cheeks were rather flushed from the heat of the house, and as she sat watching Esther, he could not help thinking, *She's the prettiest girl I ever knew.*

"Did I tell you I got a letter from Uncle Silas not long ago?" she asked. Silas was her father's brother, who lived in Richmond. "He's doing very well, but he misses Leah and me."

"Why doesn't he come here and stay with you?"

"I guess all of his friends are there. When you get to be his age, it's hard to make a move."

"It's hard at any age," Tom answered shortly.

Sarah gave him a thoughtful look. "It was hard for you to leave your home and move South, wasn't it?"

"Yes."

Seeming to recognize that he did not want to discuss the past, Sarah changed the subject.

Still later that morning Ezra crossed the yard to the walnut tree. He had been working in the garden, and his face was red from the heat. His overalls were damp with perspiration. He looked very tall and lean, and his curly brown hair stuck out from under his straw hat.

Throwing himself down beneath the tree, he poked at Esther with a finger and smiled when she laughed aloud. "Sure is hot today, ain't it, Tom?"

"Yeah, I reckon it is," Tom replied. He watched Ezra play with the baby, and he thought, *I bet Pa would like to see Esther. I wish he could.*

"How about a game of checkers?" Ezra suggested. "I'm going to wait until it cools off before I go back out there."

"All right."

The one activity that Tom engaged in was a series of checker games with Ezra. They were evenly matched and had developed a fierce rivalry.

Ezra went into the house and brought out the checkerboard. For a while they moved the red and black disks about the board. Ezra won one game and then Tom two.

When they had played the last game, Ezra said rather self-consciously, "Tom, I still been thinking about what we talked about—about getting you a new leg made."

Tom did not respond, keeping his eyes on the board.

But Ezra was encouraged even by his silence. "I tell you, I think it wouldn't be too hard. I'd like to tackle it." Ezra loved any sort of work with wood, and for a while he explained what he thought he could do.

"Of course," he said, "I don't know that much about this sort of thing, but I could find out. Why don't you and me—"

Tom looked up from the checkerboard, his dark eyes half shut. "Ezra, we talked about this, and I told you—I don't want to do it. Now just leave me alone!"

Ezra could not understand the anger in Tom. It seemed logical to him that a man should do what he could to help himself. Still, he could not go against Tom's will.

"All right, Tom," he said quietly. "It's your say."

After Ezra had picked up the board and left, Tom sat thinking. He did not understand himself. Life had changed so terribly since he had been injured. Before, he had always been excited, looking to the future. But now there seemed to be nothing for him. Nothing at all.

4

Bare Knuckles

The pleasant aroma of hair oil and lotion filled the barbershop. Rosie sat down in the chair, and the barber put a white cloth under his chin.

"Be right careful with that razor, Shorty! I can't spare to lose no blood."

Shorty Masters, who stood over six feet four, was indignant. "It ain't my habit," he grumbled, "to cut my customers up."

Rosie looked up with his innocent expression. "Well, I'm a little more particular than most, Shorty. See, I'm taking a special blood medicine I imported from Chicago. It's stuff that cost five dollars a bottle, and I can't afford to spill none of it."

Drake Bedford, who was waiting his turn, laughed aloud. "You spend every dime you get on those patent medicines, Rosie. You ought to invest your money wisely—like I do."

Rosie lifted his head and gazed at his friend. "I don't call that white lightning you drank last night a good investment." He wagged his head despairingly. "It could rot your insides. I keep telling you, Drake."

"Each man to his own poison," Drake said.

Rosie leaned back.

Taking the brush, Shorty lathered his face with thick white soap. Then he took a straight razor and expertly stropped it several times. He began to shave Rosie. "What kind of blood disease you got?"

"I don't know exactly if there's a name for it," Rosie mumbled through the suds. He waited until Shorty raked all the shaving cream off the left side of his face and had rather roughly turned his head the other way. "The ad said this here medicine would rejuvenate an Egyptian mummy, and it also promised that anyone who took it on a regular basis would never die of no blood disease."

"Five dollars a bottle—that's a pretty expensive way of staying alive!"

"I know," Rosie agreed. "But I ain't worried about it. I think my heart will give out before my blood quits. That is, if my lungs don't stop working first."

A laugh went around the barbershop, for Rosie's ailments were well advertised.

Soon talk turned to the war, and one customer awaiting his turn said, "Looks like Rosecrans is going to take the whole Union army down to Chattanooga."

"I don't reckon they need them anymore in Vicksburg," Shorty answered. "Now that Grant's whipped the Rebels down there, we can get on with this thing."

"I don't see how those Rebels hold out!" another customer observed. He laid down the paper that he had been reading. "They just keep on losing men they can't replace. They ain't no quit in them, is there?"

Rosie waited until Shorty finished shaving his upper lip. Then he said, "That fellow Grant, I seen him once. He looks like all sorts of a feller!"

"What *does* he look like?" Drake asked curiously. "Can't tell much by his pictures."

"Well, he's just a little feller, but he's got kind of a stubborn look," Rosie observed. "To me he looks like a feller that's just decided to lower his head and run it through an oak door. Whatever he sets out to do, I reckon he's going to do it."

"Well—" another customer, a Southern sympathizer, grunted "—he may have won a battle at Vicksburg, but he never run into Bobbie Lee and his boys yet. It'll be different when he does."

Shorty finished shaving Rosie, doused strong-smelling lotion over his hair, and then parted it exactly in the middle, as Rosie liked it.

"Now," Shorty said with satisfaction, "you look good enough to go to the opera!" He took the coin that Rosie handed him. "Drake, you're next!"

Drake Bedford undraped himself from the cane-bottom chair that he had tilted back against the wall. He sauntered over and plopped himself down in the barber chair.

"Just a little off around the sideburns. Do a good job, Shorty!" He grinned, and his white teeth flashed against his tanned face. "I'm going courting tonight, and I want to look good. And don't put any of that French perfume on me like you baptized Rosie with!"

"Why, that's the most expensive stuff I got in the house!"

"Well, it smells like perfume. Don't use it on me!"

Shorty carefully worked on the haircut. Drake had crisp brown hair that took a cut nicely. "You going to the box supper tonight?" the barber asked.

"Where's that?"

"Why, at the community hall. The parson got it up. The gals are all coming, bringing box suppers, and all the bachelors get to bid for their supper, and they get to eat it with the gals."

"What are they going to use the money for?" Drake asked idly.

"Oh, some missionary in Africa, I think."

Drake's eyes brightened. "I just might go to that!" He smiled around at the other customers. "The rest of you fellas might as well not get in the bidding on Miss Lori Jenkins's box. I kind of got her staked out for myself."

Grins went around the barbershop, and Shorty said, "I don't think you'll get much competition out of this bunch. The way you pounded Darrell kind of tipped off the rest of the fellas. I don't reckon Miss Lori's had another gentleman caller since you done that!"

As Rosie and Drake left the barbershop ten minutes later, Rosie said, "I think I'm getting some kind of a disease in my brain, Drake. Maybe I better go see the doc about it."

Drake laughed at his friend. "Just give me the money you'd pay him, and I'll treat you as well as he could. Save your money for that box supper. You'll want to buy you a good meal with that Reilly girl you're so sweet on."

"Ain't sure I'll live through the day!" Rosie moaned. He looked hale and hearty to Drake in the fresh morning air, but he insisted on stopping by for his almost daily visit to the doctor.

Drake arrived early at the community hall, a building also used at times for voting and for meetings of the county board. He saw that several musicians had brought their instruments. He borrowed a fiddle, and soon music filled the place.

41

Rosie wandered about, looking over the young ladies that had come with their box suppers, and encountered Sarah and Royal.

"How are you, Miss Carter?" he asked. He eyed the box in her hand and said woefully, "I'd like to bid on that box you got there, but I done spent all my money at the doctor's office. Besides, a pretty gal like you, that box will probably go for fifteen dollars. My loss!"

Royal was smiling happily. He had missed this sort of thing in the army, and the music and the voices of happy people sounded good. "I'll be glad to lend you some money, Rosie, but you may be right about Sarah here. The last time we had a box supper, the boys got into a bidding war before I even left home. I think Clem Judson and Ira Feathers just about busted themselves—it took 'em six months to work themselves out of debt, but Clem told me it was worth it."

Royal put an arm around his sister and gave her a squeeze. "Just to eat your fried chicken, Sis."

Sarah smiled back at him but said, "You go ahead and bid, Rosie. I'd be glad to have supper with you."

Royal searched the room until his eyes lighted on Lori Jenkins, talking with two other girls. "I guess Miss Lori's got my supper ready."

Rosie lifted both eyebrows. "You ain't aimin' to bid on Miss Lori's box?"

"I sure am!"

Rosie shook his head. "Don't reckon that would be the wise thing to do. You know what the Good Book says—'A wise man looketh well to his going.'"

A puzzled look came over Royal's face. "What do

you mean? That's what this is—a box supper. You're *supposed* to bid!"

"Was I you, I think I'd pick some other girl. Look over there at that one, the redhead. Now, she would do right well. Her name's Irene Campbell, and I can tell you she's a good cook. I et with her folks once, and she done the cooking. I'd advise you to bid on Irene's box."

"Rosie, I've got my mind made up to eat with Miss Lori."

Rosie scratched his head, and his homely face was mournful. "Wouldn't be very healthy!"

"You mean she can't cook?"

"I don't know about that, but the truth is—well, Drake's got *his* head set on eatin' with her. He kind of hinted that it wouldn't be prudent for anyone else to try to buy Miss Lori's box supper."

A stubborn look came over Royal's face, but he only said politely, "Well, it's for a good cause, and if Lori offers a box supper, anybody's free to bid."

Now Sarah looked troubled. "They're lots of pretty girls here, Royal!" she said. "Just choose one of them."

"Nope, it's Miss Lori for me!"

Ten minutes later, the mayor, Alvin Buckley, stood on the low platform and called for silence. "It's time for the bidding here. I know you young fellas are hungry, and these girls have got some delicious suppers packed. Now, who'll start out?"

He waited until a young lady blushingly came and stood beside him. Then he said, "I suppose you all know that Janie Hart here is famous for her fried chicken and apple pie. Wouldn't be surprised that's what's in this box. Ain't a man in the house that wouldn't like to join Miss Janie for supper. Now

43

what are my bids? One dollar—two dollars—four dollars!"

Janie was soon claimed by a short, pudgy young man, who paid six dollars for the privilege of eating supper with her. He came forward for his prize, the two went off, and the mayor started the bidding for the next box.

Royal stood quietly beside Sarah, watching as girl after girl stood by Mr. Buckley. Finally Lori Jenkins came up, and the mayor said, "And now, here is our visitor from Tennessee. What are my bids, fellas? Come on—start high!"

"Five dollars!"

Every eye turned toward Drake Bedford, who was standing slightly away from the crowd. He was wearing a light gray shirt, dark blue trousers, and highly polished boots. He looked very handsome and confident.

The news of his warning had evidently gotten around, for there were no further bids.

And then Royal said, "Ten dollars!"

A murmur went around the room, for this was a rather high bid.

The smile faded from Drake's face, and he glared at Royal. "Fifteen dollars!"

"Twenty!" Royal shouted back.

Drake seemed about to make another bid but then shook his head. "Let the soldier have the honor," he said, but there was a warning tenseness about his lips.

Royal paid for Lori's box, then took it from her hand. He said, "Now I'm going to see what a good cook you are."

Lori looked a little worried.

44

As they were at a table, beginning to eat, she said, "You heard about Drake?"

"Aw, I heard a little, but I'll risk it," Royal said. He bit into a fried chicken leg, and his eyes brightened. "This is good! Somehow I just *knew* you would be a good cook."

They ate and sat at the table talking until the musicians struck up a brisk tune.

"There's going to be a square dance," he said. "I know you can cook—let's see if you can square-dance."

For the next hour the floor was filled with square dancers. It was a time of release and enjoyment for those who had been worn down by the war. The older people lined the walls and watched the younger folks go back and forth to the calls of the tall, thin fiddler. The girls' bright dresses lent a festive air, and most of them were expert square dancers.

Royal put Drake out of his mind and enjoyed himself. He and Lori sat out some of the dances, and during those times he found that she was as witty and charming as she was pretty.

They had started back to the floor when suddenly somebody bumped into Royal, staggering him. He looked around and saw Drake Bedford. He also saw that Drake's face was flushed and that he wore an angry expression. "Sorry, Drake!" he said. "I guess I wasn't looking where I was going."

Drake wasted no time. "Come on outside—I'm going to mop up the ground with you!"

"Why would you do that?"

And then the music went silent, and everyone was listening. Somebody far back in the crowd said, "Drake's gonna whup that soldier boy! I heard him say that any man that bid on that gal's supper, he would stomp."

Mayor Buckley came up. "Now we don't want any trouble here—"

But Drake ignored him. "If you're any kind of a man," he said to Royal, "you'll come out and fight." He gave Royal a shove, sending him backward.

A mutter went around the room.

Lori said, "Drake, you're drunk!"

"No, I'm not drunk! I just want to see what kind of a sissy you've been dancing with. Well, are you coming, Royal, or not?"

Royal felt every eye upon him. He was not a young man who liked to fight. As a matter of fact, he had not been in a fight for years, but he knew suddenly that he could not back away. If he backed down from this fight, he would be labeled a coward from this day onward.

"All right, Drake. It's a mistake, but I'll come."

A smile crossed Drake's wide mouth, and he turned and walked out of the hall.

Royal felt Sarah's hand on his arm.

She whispered, "Don't do it, Royal."

"I've got to, Sis," he muttered, then threaded his way through the crowd.

The spectators made a half circle about them, and Drake said, "Anytime you're ready. I'm gonna teach you a lesson, Royal!"

"It's up to you, Drake. I don't want this fight."

Drake shook his head. "You should've thought of that before you tried to steal my girl!"

"I'm not your girl!" Lori protested.

Even as she spoke, Drake lunged forward, fast. His fist caught Royal high on the head. The impact knocked Royal back, and he sprawled in the dust.

"This won't prove anything, Drake!" Lori cried.

Drake looked at her and grinned. "It'll prove what kind of a man Royal is—which I don't think is much."

Royal got to his feet, his head pounding. He put his fists up and advanced, once again thinking how he hated to fight.

He struck out at Drake, who easily dodged and smashed his right fist into Royal's mouth, drawing blood. A woman's voice cried out sharply, and Royal could not tell if it was Sarah's or Lori's. Then he found himself being hammered backward once more. He swung again and again, but his blows were ineffective. And Drake, an expert with his fists, landed one after another.

As from a distance Royal heard Rosie say, "I wish Drake wouldn't do stuff like this. It ain't fittin'!"

He heard Sarah cry out, "Can't you *stop* it, Rosie!"

"I won't let it go on too long. Drake ain't really mean. He'll only go so far."

But this time Drake seemed intent on punishing Royal, and soon the soldier had been knocked to the ground three times. He got up slower each time, his face flushed and bleeding. He knew he had no chance at all. Everyone could see that.

Drake advanced to continue the fight, but just then Rosie stepped out. "I reckon that's enough, Drake!"

Drake turned angrily to face him. "Maybe you want to take it up, Rosie!"

Rosie looked like a shambling, ineffectual figure, but he was as well-known for his fists as Drake himself. He said almost lazily, "That's your say, Drake. You done proved you can outfight this soldier boy, and that's as far as it goes. If you want

47

more, then I guess I'll give you the best we got at the ranch."

Drake stared at Rosie, as though considering lunging at him. But then he laughed. Slapping Rosie on the shoulder, he said, "No, I don't guess I will." He looked back at Royal, who stood dazed, not fully understanding what was happening. "Stay away from my girl, Royal, and it will be all right!"

As Drake walked away, Lori came up to Royal. She touched his bleeding mouth and said quietly, "Come inside—I'll help you clean your face." She led him through the crowd, still buzzing and humming with talk and excitement.

She sat him down in the back room where the county board usually met privately. There was a pitcher of water on a table, and she filled a basin quickly. Then, using her handkerchief, she bathed his face.

"Well!" he said ruefully. "I guess I showed that I'm not much of a man."

"Don't be silly!" Lori said. "You showed that you're not a brawler or a prizefighter."

But Royal felt ashamed of his poor showing. "I couldn't stand up against him, Lori."

"You haven't spent your life picking fights," she said. She dabbed at the cuts on his face and then cocked her head. "Well, are you still going to come calling on me?"

There was a challenge in her voice and in her eyes.

Royal grinned, though it hurt his lips. "I guess I will. Sure, I will! How about supper at your house tomorrow? I didn't get enough of your cooking."

Lori smiled. "You come. I'll make it right with my uncle and aunt."

On the way home, Sarah said to Royal, "You're not going to see Lori again, are you?"

"You know I am! A fella can't hide in a hole because another man tells him what to do."

"What will you do if he beats you up again?"

"I don't know. But I know one thing—I'm going to see Miss Lori. Whatever it takes!"

5
Old-Time Religion

Rosie held the large brown bottle up to the light and stared at it critically. Closing one eye, he evaluated the contents, then removed the top and took a sip.

"Wow! That's right strong stuff. Here—smell it, Drake."

Drake, who had been reading a newspaper, turned his head just as Rosie shoved the concoction under his nose. Jerking back, he gasped. "What in the world *is* that stuff?"

Rosie took the bottle back and admired it. "This here is Dr. Mayfield's All-around, Cure-all, Metaphysical Tonic."

Drake by this time was accustomed to Rosie's experimentation with patent medicine. "Why do you waste your money on that stuff? You're healthy as a horse!"

Rosie gave his friend a reproachful look. "Now, you know I'm not well, Drake! Why, if I didn't take care of myself, I'd be dead before suppertime!" He took a deep breath and lifted the bottle to his lips again. His Adam's apple moved up and down, and when he lowered the bottle his face was red. "Whew! That's powerful medicine. Anything that tastes *that* bad has to be good!"

Drake went back to his newspaper. The two had been sitting on the front porch of their rooming house, watching people stroll by. It was a warm

Saturday morning. They had risen early and had consumed a huge breakfast of pancakes at the boardinghouse table.

Now Rosie said lazily, "It looks like your courtship of Lori ain't prospering too much, Drake."

"Just give me time."

"Well, the fact is that you probably ain't *got* too much time. The way I understand it, she's just visiting here. Won't be here forever," Rosie observed.

Throwing down his newspaper in disgust, Drake stared out at a family going by—a husband and wife with six children, stair-stepped down from a boy of thirteen or fourteen to a little one barely able to toddle. He watched until they passed the boardinghouse and then admitted, "To tell the truth, Rosie, I never met a girl quite like her. She's pretty straight-laced, though—goes to church all the time."

"Well, a smart fellow like you shouldn't have much trouble figuring out how to handle that."

"What do you mean?"

"I mean, if she's a churchgoing girl, all you have to do is go to church."

A look of displeasure crossed Drake's face. "I'm not much for churchgoing!" he snapped.

"I reckon that's gospel." Rosie grinned. "I ain't never known of you hittin' the glory trail. Why don't you just give up on her? She seems to be favoring Royal Carter anyway."

Although Rosie may only have guessed at it, he had hit on a sore spot with Drake Bedford. The young man was accustomed to quick victories over girls. His sleek good looks, his charm, and his musical ability had always made him highly sought after. It had given Drake satisfaction to whip Royal in a fistfight—but for some reason the results had not been satisfactory. He continued to pursue Lori Jenkins, but she had not been as receptive as other young ladies.

"You're a funny fellow, Drake," Rosie said idly. "You always want what you can't have. I remember that horse you wanted down in Shelby County. You remember that steel gray pacer? There was plenty of horses as good as him, but the fella wouldn't sell. So what did you do? Why, you had to move heaven and earth to get that one horse! I always did think you made a mistake."

Guiltily Drake replied, "That *was* a good horse. I won quite a few races on him."

"Aw, you never got your money back. You know that. You're just the kind of hairpin who *has* to have what somebody tells him he can't. I bet when your mama wanted you to do something like bring in the wood, she'd say, 'Drake, don't you bring in the wood!' And then you'd go bring it in, just to show her you wouldn't be told."

"Don't be foolish!" Actually, Drake realized, Rosie's estimate of him was not far wrong, and he decided to change the subject.

"It looks like the fighting is heating up." He motioned down at the newspaper. "The South looked pretty good—winning at Chancellorsville and Second Bull Run—but they don't look so good now. After Gettysburg and then losing at Vicksburg— well, this war might not last too long."

"Wouldn't be too sure about that! Those folks down South are serious. They'll fight down to the last man." But then Rosie changed the subject. "Why don't you and me ride into Lexington? We haven't been there in a spell. And we've got a little cash."

But Drake shook his head stubbornly. "I've got a few chores to do around Pineville. Maybe later, Rosie."

Rosie squinted with one eye as if examining a specimen in a laboratory. "I can read you like a book. As a matter of fact, I ain't no fortune-teller, but I can tell you right now what you aim to do, Drake."

"I don't think so!"

"You're gonna ask that girl to go to church just like I told ya." Rosie nodded wisely, got to his feet, and stretched hugely. "Reckon I'll take a walk, then. I ought to be able to make a mile or two without passing out. Maybe."

As Rosie ambled off, Drake wondered how a man as strong and healthy as A. B. Rose could be so concerned about his health. As soon as his friend was out of sight, he got to his feet and left the boardinghouse in the opposite direction.

Pineville was a small town containing no more than four or five hundred full-time residents, and the Jenkins house was only a short walk. Drake stopped in front of the two-story white frame building, looked over the white picket fence, and was pleased to see Lori on the front porch.

He opened the gate, walked up to the steps, and lifted his hat. "Good morning, Lori." He smiled. "You're up early for a Saturday."

"I've got a lot of work to do. I have to help my aunt clean house today. No work tomorrow—Sunday, you know."

"Yes, I know. I came by to ask you if I might take you to church."

Drake's words were innocent enough, but Lori gave him an odd look. "I didn't know you went to church, Drake."

"Whatever's given me a bad reputation like that?" Drake knew he was looking very handsome that morning. He wore a blue shirt with buttons in cavalry style, a pair of light gray trousers, and his boots—as usual—were black and glossy and shone in the July sunlight. His crisp hair was neatly cut, and his teeth looked very white against his tanned skin. "Maybe I haven't gone to church as much as I should, but I'd like to go tomorrow. Why don't you take pity on me?"

Lori thought for a moment and nodded her head. "All right. My uncle and aunt would be glad to have you join us," she said.

So he would be going with the family, not just with her. Drake had expected this, and it was fine with him. He knew he had to start somewhere. He said, "I'll be here a little early. Give my best to your uncle and aunt."

He turned and walked away.

Lori watched him go, thinking, *It's a shame to be so suspicious of a young man—but he's gotten quite a bad reputation.* A small smile turned up the corners of her lips. *Well, it won't hurt him to hear a sermon.*

Sunday morning dawned, and Drake was at the Jenkins house by nine o'clock as he had promised. Lori welcomed him, and he sat for some time with Hamilton Jenkins, her uncle, while Mrs. Jenkins and Lori applied final touches to their costumes.

Mr. Jenkins, a tall, bluff man with a pair of direct blue eyes, ran a hardware store. If he had a low opinion of Drake, thinking him rather wild, he let none of this show. "We're glad to have you go to church with us, Drake," he said. "I think you'll like the preacher."

"I'm sure I will, Mr. Jenkins," Drake said politely. He was wearing a light gray suit today with a snow-white shirt and a black string tie.

As he spoke, the two women entered, and he stood. "Well, we men sometimes have to wait for the ladies," he observed with smile, "but they are worth waiting for."

Both Lori and her Aunt Mae smiled at the compliment. Drake had a way of saying such things that made them appear not to be flattery but the simple truth.

"Why, thank you, Drake," Lori said. She was wearing a simple white dress with blue trim at the neck and on the sleeves. The skirt fell to the tops of a pair of dark blue shoes.

Her aunt had on a more serious brown dress, and both women wore hats.

"Well, we'd best be going," Mr. Jenkins said. His wife took his arm, and he led the way out of the house.

Lori walked alongside Drake, and soon the foursome arrived at a white frame building with a steeple that pierced the sky. It was a well-built, snug church, not large but sturdy.

Inside, Drake saw that the walnut pews were well made. They had been varnished, and they gleamed in the sunlight that poured in through the tall windows running down each side. The floor was solid pine, also highly polished.

The Jenkinses drew attention as they took seats close to the front. Drake would have preferred the back of the church, but he had no choice. Sitting down beside Lori, he felt a nudge and looked back to see an elderly lady with pure white hair offering him a hymnbook.

"Thank you, ma'am," he said, and smiled at her.

At the front of the church was a raised platform, covered with wine-colored carpet. There was a sturdy pulpit, a table bearing a pitcher and a glass, and two chairs—one on either side of the pulpit. One chair was occupied by a heavyset man, whose face was red from a collar that seemed too tight. This was the song leader, Drake soon learned. The other was the minister, he supposed—a tall, gray-haired, dignified-looking man of about fifty.

The song leader got up. "We'll now lift our voices in song to the Lord."

Drake shared his songbook with Lori, which gave him an opportunity to lean closer to her. Despite Rosie's words about his lack of church-going, he had been to revival meetings and was familiar with most of the songs, for the congregation sang such old favorites as "When I Survey the Wondrous Cross."

Drake's beautiful tenor rose above the rest of the congregation, almost seeming to be a solo. Admiring looks came from many in his vicinity, and when the song was over Lori whispered, "You have such a beautiful voice, Drake! I'm glad to hear you using it to praise the Lord."

Her words made him feel a little ashamed. *I shouldn't be doing this,* he thought. *There are other ways to court a girl. Somehow this isn't right.*

After the song service, the leader took his seat, and the pastor stood up. His name was Brother Morgan, and he had a pleasant baritone voice. There was little nonsense about him—no stories, no jokes. At once he opened his worn black Bible and began to read from Luke, chapter 15.

Looking up from the Bible, Brother Morgan said quietly but in a firm tone, "Our subject this morning is salvation—something every man and every woman must consider. The Bible from beginning to end states that all men are lost. The book of Romans says that 'all have sinned and come short of the glory of God.' That same book tells us that 'the wages of sin is death, but the gift of God is eternal life.' You all are aware that the Bible speaks of a place of eternal fire. You also have heard me say, many times, that heaven is the place where we live forever in fellowship with God.

"This morning I have chosen one of the most dramatic pictures of salvation in the entire New Testament—the story of the Prodigal Son."

He settled himself behind the pulpit and began to tell how the young man in the story had deliberately thrown away his inheritance. He painted vivid word pictures of what it meant to go away from God.

Drake had not planned to listen and at first had been more conscious of Lori's sitting beside him than he was of the sermon. However, he soon found himself caught up in the preacher's message.

Brother Morgan told how the young man began to go wrong. Here he drew on his imagination and spoke of the ways that young men and women go wrong at the present time. They sometimes begin to drink and gamble and associate with low companions, he said.

Drake kept a straight face, but he thought, *I think Brother Morgan's been reading my mail.* He stiffened as the message grew more pointed.

Finally the preacher described the end of the young man—he was reduced to eating with hogs.

"Sin always brings us to a sad end," Brother Morgan said, his voice rising. "It is never unpaid for. Whatever a man sows, that must he also reap. If you sow corn, you will reap corn; if you sow wheat, you will reap wheat; and if you sow sin, you will reap sin's result: death and hell."

Drake could not turn off his thoughts and ignore the sermon as he had often done before. With relief, he finally sensed the conclusion coming.

"And here is this young man," Brother Morgan said. "He's lost everything. The Scripture says that he 'came to himself.' He remembered what home was like and in desperation said, 'I will arise and go to my father, and will say to him, Father, I have sinned . . .'"

Brother Morgan looked out over the congregation, and his eyes met, perhaps by accident, those of Drake. "That's what every young man and young woman who's gone away from God needs to do. Each one needs to say, 'I will arise and go to my Father.'"

Drake wanted to break his eyes away, but the eyes of the preacher were locked with his.

Brother Morgan said gently, "When he returned, he saw his house far away. Then he saw his father. And the old man who had been so wronged by this boy—what did he do? He ran to meet him. The boy began to confess his wrong, but his father said, 'No, you're my son, who was lost and now is found.'

"Jesus Christ is God's way of making things right between Himself and His erring sons and daughters. I invite you to look to Jesus this morning and do as this young man did—repent of your sins and arise and come to your Father."

There was a rustling as the congregation stood to sing a hymn.

Drake felt strangely moved by the sermon—so moved in fact that his hands trembled holding the songbook, and Lori looked up at him.

The preacher was stationed at the front door as the congregation filed out, and when Drake passed by, Brother Morgan took his hand.

Drake felt the minister's strong grip. "Fine sermon, Pastor," he muttered.

"Thank you, my friend." Brother Morgan held on for a moment and said so quietly that no one but Drake could have heard, "God is waiting for you, young man. Don't pass Him by!"

Drake looked up, startled, and then ducked his head and left.

The Jenkinses insisted that he take dinner with them, and Drake availed himself of the opportunity. Afterward he sat on the front porch with the family, talking.

When Mr. and Mrs. Jenkins went into the house for a nap, Lori asked, "Did you enjoy the service, Drake?"

"Fine preacher," Drake admitted. "Don't know if I ever heard better."

"Yes, I think so too."

Then he said, "I'd like to do this again—with you, I mean."

Lori gave him an odd look. "I think that would be fine, Drake—but it won't be possible."

"What do you mean? What's wrong?"

"Oh, nothing's wrong, but I'll be going home to Chattanooga later this week."

Drake felt suddenly depressed. He said lamely, "Lori, can't you stay a *little* longer? We're just getting to know each other."

"I'd like to stay longer," she admitted, "but my parents wrote that they need me at home right away. My sister's ill, and I need to help take care of her."

The rest of the visit was not happy for Drake.

When he finally rose and she put out her hand to say good-bye, he said, "I've never felt about a girl as I do about you, Lori."

"Oh, you've said *that* before."

Since this was true, Drake flushed slightly. "Well, perhaps I have," he admitted, "but I *mean* it this time. I want to see you again. Will you write to me?"

"Of course, if you write me first."

Drake wanted to kiss her good-bye, but he knew that was impossible. He picked up his hat and left the porch, then turned to wave.

She waved back, and he felt even worse.

Later that afternoon Rosie walked out onto the boardinghouse front porch, took one look at Drake, and asked, "What's the matter with you? You look like an accident going somewhere to happen."

"Nothing's wrong with me!"

Rosie stretched his lanky form over one of the porch chairs. "That gal—she's really got you going, don't she?"

At first Drake did not answer. Then he looked at his friend. "I'll tell you the truth, Rosie—I'm in love with her."

He saw Rosie's look of disbelief. Drake Bedford had courted many girls, and Rosie was aware of his record.

"Well, it won't hurt you to suffer a little bit, I reckon," Rosie said. "You've brought enough grief to a whole passel of young ladies."

"You don't believe me, but it's true." Determination came into Drake's eyes. "Somehow I'm going to see more of her—watch and see if I don't!"

6
A Hasty Decision

Ezra Payne went into town on the last day of July, a Thursday, to buy supplies. He stopped by the hardware store, made a few purchases, then walked on down to Hank's General Store. As he entered, he found A. B. Rose arguing with the owner over a purchase.

Ezra grinned as he listened to the tall young man declare that the patent medicine he held was priced too high.

"I can't help the prices," the storekeeper said. "You'll just have to pay it or leave it here."

Rosie reached into his pocket and pulled out a few coins. "I just ain't got enough—you'll have to trust me for it."

Ezra said, "I'll be glad to float you a loan, Rosie." He liked Rosie, and, despite their different points of view on religion, they were fairly good friends.

Rosie turned around, and a smile lighted up his homely face. "Well, now, that's handsome of you, Ezra. Just lend me a dollar, will you? I think I've got the rest."

He took the money from Ezra and handed it to the storekeeper. "There you are, Mr. Miles." Then he held up the package and admired the showy red and yellow advertising on the outside. "This ought to do it, sure enough."

"What's that for, Rosie?" Ezra asked, winking at Mr. Miles.

"Well, it's going to cure my liver disease," Rosie said solemnly. He tore the top open and pulled out an enormous pill. "Any pill this big ought to be good." He popped one into his mouth. Almost strangling, he forced it down, then gasped, "There. Do your work down there and get that liver straightened up!"

Ezra said, "I'll buy you a root beer, Rosie, after I get through with my business here."

"That'd be mighty fine. It'll settle this pill down a little bit—maybe mollify it."

Ezra bought the items on his list, and as Mr. Miles put them into a box, he picked up two bottles of root beer and handed one to Rosie. "Get on the outside of this, Rosie!" He grinned. "Maybe it'll cure something for you."

"My Uncle Seedy, he always said root beer was good to keep off malaria. He must've drunk seven or eight gallons a year."

"Did he ever get malaria?"

"Just three or four times. But he always said he might have had it a hundred times—or maybe he might have died of it—if he hadn't drunk all that root beer."

They sat down and sipped their soft drinks. Abruptly Ezra said, "I guess Drake lost out this time."

"Yep, I reckon he did, but he says he's gonna keep on courting that gal."

"I don't guess he'll be courting her now—she's going home to Tennessee." Ezra sampled the root beer again and looked at it appreciatively. "This sure is good stuff! I wish I could afford to drink it every day!" He took another sip. "Guess Royal will have a clear field now."

"But he won't be able to court her either."

"Yes, he will! He's in Rosecrans's army, and everybody knows where *they're* headed."

"Why, that's right! They're headed for Chattanooga to settle old General Bragg and the Confederates down there."

"That's right! So I expect Royal will be able to go courtin' after all. He told me Miss Lori lives just outside of town, and the army will be stationed there for a while."

"Well, I'll be dogged!" Rosie grinned. "This looks like one time Drake's going to get his eye waxed as far as a pretty girl is concerned. I never thought I'd see the day!"

Later in the day Rosie encountered Drake in the restaurant, drinking coffee and staring into space.

"Well, this is one time you lost out!" he announced with satisfaction, plunking down beside him. It pleased Rosie to see Drake beat out once in a while. He admired the young man but thought he was a little conceited.

"What do you mean by that?" Drake demanded.

"I'm talking about Miss Lori."

"What about her?"

"She lives just outside of Chattanooga."

"I know that. What about it?"

"Why, Chattanooga—that's where Rosecrans is taking the Union army, and guess who's in that army?" Rosie grinned broadly. "Royal Carter, that's who." He punched Drake a sharp blow on the shoulder. "You sure took second place this time! I hate to get on a man when he's down, but dog my cats if it ain't time you learned what it's like to come in second, Drake. It does a man good to be humbled once in a while."

Drake straightened up and stared at him. Then his face settled into a stubborn look. He said nothing but sat drinking coffee while Rosie ate his meal.

Finally Rosie finished and tossed down his napkin. "Looks like the dinner's on you. I forgot to tell you I don't have any money. My treat next time." He strolled off but gave one parting shot over his shoulder. "Reckon it's right romantic down there in Chattanooga. Mountains and rivers. Wouldn't be surprised but what Royal doesn't do some high-powered courtin'. Yessiree, they're going to make a mighty happy couple!"

Drake stared after Rosie angrily, then looked down at his empty cup.

The waitress came by. She was a short, heavyset, plain girl—and she was hopelessly enamored by Drake Bedford.

"Would you like some more coffee, Drake?"

"No, Lucille." He got to his feet, threw down some coins on the table, and walked out without another word.

Lucille picked up the change, then turned back to the kitchen. "You don't have to be so spiteful about it!" she muttered.

In the middle of the afternoon, Royal and Lori came into the restaurant for ice cream. His face was still slightly puffy around one scar.

"I sure do like ice cream," Royal said. He lifted his spoon and waved at the waitress. "Bring me one more bowl of this, Lucille, then don't let me have any more, no matter how much I beg for it!"

Lori sat across the table from him. She had lifted a spoonful of vanilla ice cream but paused and scolded, "You're going to kill yourself, Royal—eating five bowls of ice cream!"

"An agreeable way to die!" Royal sighed. "I'm not likely to get any ice cream where I'm going. So I've got to eat enough to make it last."

"You're going to hate going back to the army, I suppose."

"Oh, no," he said. "It's just something that has to be done. There's no point in moaning and groaning about doing your duty. Lots of the fellows do, but that just makes it worse."

"I think that's a good way to look at things," Lori answered. "Sometimes I spend more time complaining about having to do the ironing than the ironing takes."

He thought she was looking very pretty today. She wore a yellow dress that suited her well.

They talked about the army as Royal finished his last bowl of ice cream.

"It must be nice to be an officer," she said.

"I suppose so, but they have lots of responsibility."

Then Lori said, "I'm going to miss you, Royal."

Royal looked at her, his warm brown eyes glowing. "You're not going to miss me as much as you think. The army will be somewhere around the Chattanooga area for some time. Everybody knows there's going to be fighting. I'll find some way to get to see you. Maybe you can come out to the camp. We have revival meetings most every time we stay at one place for a spell."

"I'd like that." She started to say something else, but then her eyes flew to the door. "Why, hello, Drake."

Drake Bedford came over to their table. "Mind if I join you?" he asked, his eyes going from Lori to Royal, as though half expecting Royal to tell him to move on.

"Why, sure. Sit down, Drake," Royal said. "Lori was just telling me she's leaving for Chattanooga tomorrow."

"Yes, I know." Drake shook his head when the waitress approached. "Nothing for me this time, Lucille." As soon as she turned away, he smiled at Lori. "Hope you have a safe trip back to Tennessee —and an easy one."

"I wish I didn't have to go, but my parents insist."

"I know—it's too bad about your sister. I hope she'll get better soon!" Drake said easily.

"I'll be leaving right away too, Drake," Royal said. "Just want you to know there's no hard feelings about the fight."

"Why, that's decent of you to say so, Royal. Most fellows wouldn't be able to put it out of their minds that easy."

"I don't believe in holding grudges."

"Well, I don't either, and it's a good thing you feel that way since we'll probably be pretty close to each other for a while."

Both Royal and Lori looked blankly at him.

"What do you mean?" Royal asked. "I'll be leaving with my regiment right away."

Drake smiled at Lori. "I guess you'll have to put up with me a little bit more. I'll be coming to call on you when you get back home, Lori."

67

"In Tennessee? But how can you do that, Drake?"

"The U.S. Government is sending me down that way on a business trip." Drake glanced over at Royal. "The truth is, Royal, I've joined up with your outfit. I'll be in your company, as a matter of fact. In the Washington Blues. I'm the newest recruit."

For a moment Royal could not believe him.

"You're not serious, are you, Drake?" Lori exclaimed.

"I was never more serious in my life. I'm already sworn in. Be getting a uniform tomorrow. I'll be a private, and you'll be the veteran, Royal—so you'll be the boss."

Royal at once understood what Drake was doing, and he was appalled. "Drake," he said slowly, "I wish you hadn't done this."

"Why not? You're not afraid of a little competition, are you?"

"I wasn't meaning that," Royal insisted. He leaned forward earnestly. "Being in the army is a serious thing. It's not something you do just to go courting. In the first place, you don't know for sure that we'll *be* in Chattanooga."

"Oh, everybody knows that," Drake said airily. "That's where the Reb army in Tennessee is, and we got to roust them out. Just read the papers."

"They might pull out. We might be sent to fight around Richmond instead. A lot of things can happen."

But Drake did not pay any heed. He turned to Lori again. "That sure is a pretty dress you've got on," he said. "I hope you wear it when I come calling down in Tennessee."

He rose then and laughed at the expression on Royal's face. "Don't worry about it, Professor. You and me, we'll have a time running the Rebs out of Chattanooga. Then we can go and sit on Miss Lori's front porch." He laughed again and walked away.

"He's so impulsive!" Lori almost whispered.

"Yes, he is," Royal said, "and he's going to find out that soldiering's not quite as easy as he thinks." He frowned. "Drake's always had his own way. Nobody could ever tell him anything. And now he's going to find out he's only one more private in a mighty big army. They've got ways of making life miserable for you."

Lori leaned over and touched his hand. "But *you* won't, will you? Most men would, but not you. Drake needs help. He doesn't know God, and he's headed for a fall. Kind of watch out for him, will you, Royal?"

Royal took her hand and held it and smiled encouragingly. "I'll do the best I can—but most men don't pay any more attention to the sergeant than the rules say they have to."

The next day Rosie surprised Drake, just as Rosie had been surprised himself by the news that Drake was joining the army. As Drake was packing, Rosie entered the room the two shared and announced, "Well, I can't let you go off by yourself to this here fight. Reckon I'll just go along too."

Drake looked up, mouth open. "What'd you say, Rosie?"

Rosie pulled out a suitcase and began loading his enormous supply of pills and potions and bottles into it.

"I've been meanin' to sign up for quite a while—this here war is the biggest thing that is ever gonna be in our time. Otherwise, don't reckon I could rightly face my grandchildren when they said, 'What did you do in the war, Grandpa?' I'll go along and be sure you're all right."

Rosie held up a large blue bottle and scowled. "I'm about out of Dr. Zokor's Famous Kidney Medicine," he said. "Have to get some on the way."

Drake actually was glad to hear of Rosie's enlistment. He would've missed his friend a great deal. He slapped the gangly boy on the back. "We'll show 'em how to soldier, won't we?"

"To tell the truth, I don't expect to live long enough to get to the battlefield. But in case I do kick the bucket, I want you to bury me proper, wherever we are."

Drake merely laughed. He went back and began sorting through his clothes. "We'll be too busy burying Rebs for me to bury you," he said. The idea of putting on a uniform thrilled him. He looked around the room. "We'll have to get rid of most of our stuff," he said. "Uncle Sam is going to feed and clothe us for the next few months."

Rosie, however, was looking down at his supply of medicines. "I hope they got good doctors in this here regiment. My condition needs good medical care."

7

Home to Tennessee

On September 4, the Union army crossed the Tennessee River toward Chattanooga. Their plan was to get behind the Confederates, cut off their supplies, and bottle them up in the city. The Southerners then would be forced either to fight their way out, surrender, or starve.

The sun had gone down by the time campfires were lit, and soon the cooks were busy roasting beef for the army's evening meal. Royal stood looking about the company, pleased with the showing the Washington Blues had made.

Jay Walters came by. "Well, Professor, when do you think we'll catch up with the Rebels?"

"Don't call me that—at least not until we're back home."

"Aw, sorry about that, Royal."

At that moment they were joined by Walter Beddows, also a member of A Company from Pineville. The three of them had fished together, had hunted together, and now had fought together in earlier battles.

Royal looked at them fondly. "You know," he said quietly, "it's good to have you fellows here. Good to have men you know on each side of you when the fighting starts."

"You're right about that," Jay said. He was tall, very thin, and had light brown eyes and reddish-brown hair. He glanced over to where Rosie and

Drake sat beside the fire, watching the cooks prepare supper. "Now there are five of us in the company from Pineville."

"That Rosie, though," Jay said. "He's always taking medicine. I didn't know a man could have so many ailments!"

Royal grinned, looking at the lanky Rosie, who was spreading his hands as he told some tall tale to the soldiers who had gathered about him. "He sure is a talker, but I think he's as healthy as a horse. I think he's a hypochondriac."

Jay Walters stared at him. "Is that anything like an Episcopalian?"

"No, you ignoramus!" Beddows exclaimed. "That means a fellow who always thinks he's sick."

"Well," Jay said, "that's Rosie all right. Still, he's a good soldier. But Drake, I don't know about him."

Silence fell over the small group. Royal figured they were all thinking the same thing. Drake, as far as the physical part of soldiering was concerned, had proved to be an outstanding new recruit. He was strong, an excellent shot with a musket, and his eyesight was keen enough to make him a valuable asset. On the other hand, he was not as popular as Rosie, for he was constantly boasting about what would happen to the Rebels when the Union army caught up with them.

"I wish he'd soften up on his bragging a little bit, for a fact," Walter Beddows mused. "He's not doing himself any favors with the rest of the company."

Royal knew that this was true. He had not said anything to Drake yet, but he was sure that Bedford was in for trouble.

Soon the call for mess came, and the troops gathered around with their plates and tin cups.

Royal took his helping of roast beef and bread and coffee, then sat down with the other members of the squad.

The cooks had done a good job, and Rosie had urged one to overload his plate. Now he sat down with a small mountain of beef.

"That's a lot of beef for a sick man, Rosie!" Walter Beddows teased.

"Well, you know, Walter," Rosie said, nodding wisely, "every meal I eat, it's like the fellow that was about to be hanged. You know when they hang fellows, they give 'em anything they want for their last meal." He picked up a huge forkful of meat, chewed on it, and swallowed with a shudder. "Way I figure it, with a man in my condition, every meal might be his last."

Murmurs went around the campfire, and smiles were hidden behind hands. The squad was well aware of Rosie's peculiarities.

Drake ate with a healthy appetite and, putting his plate down, went for another cup of coffee. When he came back, he sat down and looked around him. "Feel sorry for those Rebels," he said with a grin. "They'll never know what hit 'em after the Washington Blues get through with 'em."

Royal felt it was time to put some sort of brake on this recruit. "Drake," he said, "I think you've got the wrong idea about those Confederates."

"How's that?" Drake challenged.

"Well, you seem to think all we have to do is say, 'Boo,' and they'll turn around and head for Richmond."

Drake leaned back on an elbow and sipped his coffee. He had an air of supreme confidence. "After

Gettysburg, I reckon we proved who's got the best army."

"I'm not sure of that at all," Royal said. "I talked to Tom Majors. He doesn't like to talk about the war, but he told us about how his outfit went across that field right into enemy fire. Well, those Southern fellows are fighting for their homes. They're not going to turn around and run just because we show up at Chattanooga."

"Aw, Royal," Drake scoffed, "don't be an old woman."

Later, when Drake Bedford and Rosie were alone, Rosie said, "You know, Drake, we're newcomers to this here army business. Might be best if we didn't brag so much."

Drake stared with dissatisfaction at Rosie. "I know they think I'm a braggart, but I'll show 'em when the time comes. So will you, Rosie. We been out on enough hunts together—coons and deer—we know how to hit a target."

Rosie's homely face was unsmiling. "Yeah," he said, "but coon and deer—they don't shoot back."

However, Drake paid no attention to him.

The next night he got out his fiddle and began to play. Fiddling was his chief contribution to the march. All soldiers loved music, and the Washington Blues were no exception. Drake could play anything well, it seemed, and often joined in the singing himself.

He began to sing a song called "Come in Out of the Draft."

The draft—or "conscription," as it was called—was practiced in both South and North. Volunteers often did not fill the gaps, so men had to be forced

to enlist in the army. It was possible to hire a sub-
stitute to go in your place, or sometimes simply getting married got a man off the hook. In any case,
the "conscripts" were looked down on by the rest of
the soldiers.

The song went:

> As it was rather warm,
>   I thought the other day
> I'd find some cooler place
>   the summer months to stay.
> I had not long been gone
>   when a paper to me came,
> And in the list of conscripts
>   I chanced to see my name.
> I showed it to my friends,
>   and they all laughed,
> They said, "How are you, Conscript?
>   Come in out of the draft.
>
> I tried to get a wife,
>   I tried to get a "Sub,"
> But what I next shall do,
>   now, really, is the "rub."
> My money's almost gone,
>   and I am nearly daft;
> Will someone tell me what to do
>   to get out of the draft?
> I've asked friends all around,
>   but at me they all laughed
> And said, "How are you, Conscript?
>   Come in out of the draft.

Lieutenant Smith stopped by and listened, and a
smile touched his lips. However, when Drake

stopped singing and began to talk again about what wonderful things the Blues were going to do, his smile disappeared.

Later the lieutenant said to Royal, "Carter, what about Drake Bedford? Pretty much of a boaster, isn't he?"

Royal was embarrassed. "Well, sir, he's just a new recruit. He'll calm down after he smells battle smoke a time or two."

Lieutenant Smith cocked his head. "I like to see men with spirit and confidence," he said. "Maybe your friend has it. He's from your hometown, isn't he?"

"Yes, sir. I've known him a long time."

"Is he a good soldier?"

"Yes, sir, he's a good shot, strong, can march all day. I'd have to say he's a real asset to the company."

"Well, we need men who believe in themselves."

"At least he's that, sir."

The Union army pushed its way toward Chattanooga. General Bragg evacuated the city and moved his forces farther south to wait for the Union troops.

The Northern general misinterpreted this as a retreat and decided to pursue the Confederates. What he should have known was that it was highly dangerous to go charging into an unknown situation.

His Army of the Cumberland formed three wings. Unfortunately, they got separated from each other, and communications broke down. Then General Rosecrans awoke to the fact that this enemy was not fleeing. He realized the dangerous position in which his army was placed and that he was heavily outnumbered.

Time flew by. Everyone was waiting. How long would the Rebels wait to attack? The longer they waited, the dimmer their chances. Finally, on September 18, Bragg gave the order to strike the following morning.

8

Battle Fury

On September 19 the Battle of Chickamauga began. It turned out to be one of the most confusing battles of the war.

In order to attack the Union forces, the Confederates had to cross Chickamauga Creek. They held most of the bridges, so they rushed ahead, and soon three-fourths of General Bragg's army was west of the stream.

The Union army pushed ahead also. The area was densely wooded, and the Washington Blues stumbled through undergrowth that clawed at their uniforms. It scratched their hands and faces, and by the time their front lines were stretched about six miles through the woods, all the members of Royal's company were worn out.

All except Drake Bedford. His face was alight with excitement. His eyes gleamed, and he looked every inch a soldier as he edged past the battle line.

"Come back here, Drake!" Royal said roughly.

Drake looked ahead into the growing darkness where the Confederate troops no doubt lay. "I bet we could catch 'em off guard if we charge right now," he said.

"Well, you go tell General Rosecrans all about it," Jay Walters said. He plopped down on the ground, his back against a tree, breathing hard. "As for me, I'm willing to wait a spell."

"Be cold rations tonight, boys," Royal announced.

Before a battle, the Union troops always stashed three days' supply of rations in their knapsacks. Sometimes the Confederate spies knew exactly when they were going into battle by this sign.

Now the men scattered and ate, and soon a full moon began to rise like a silver pock-marked disk. Drake got out his fiddle and began to play "Lorena."

After he had played a few more tunes, Walter Beddows suggested, "How about a hymn or two? I always did love the old hymns."

"Don't know any," Drake said rather shortly.

He did in fact know more than one hymn, but he stubbornly refused to admit it. Since hearing that sermon on the Prodigal Son back in Pineville, he'd had a nagging inside. He could not forget the minister's eyes locking onto his. Now as he toyed with the fiddle and then played a short Scottish melody, he thought again of the man's words as he'd passed out the church door—*God is waiting for you. . . . Don't pass Him by.*

Drake was troubled by thoughts that he had never had before. In the army it was inevitable that men would talk about death. He himself never alluded to it, but as the familiar sounds of the camp rose about him—a mumbling around other campfires, a cavalry troop passing in the rear, a sharp command from an officer—he suddenly thought, *What if I did die tomorrow in the battle?* Quickly he put the thought away and began to play something cheerful.

Across the campfire from him, Jay Walters talked with Sgt. Ira Pickens, a tall, lean young man with brown eyes and bushy black hair. He was a friend of Leah's, having become acquainted with her when she accompanied her father on one of his trips.

"Looks like we're gonna see some action tomorrow, Jay," Ira said.

"I reckon so." Jay was flanked on the other side by Walter Beddows. The two stuck close together, and usually Royal was not far off.

Ira looked over to where the new recruits were whispering among themselves, and he grinned. "Reckon those fellows are anxious to see the elephant"—the term the soldiers used when referring to seeing action. "Me, I'm not so anxious," he said. "From what I hear, there's about as many of them as there is of us. And when them Southern fellas get stirred up, they're just like a swarm of hornets, and they never know when to quit."

"I hope we give a good account of ourselves," Jay said. "It's been a long war, and we seen lots of fellas go down."

"I reckon there'll be some more of us go down tomorrow," Beddows said.

He made the comment without a sign of fear, but his remark touched Drake. He turned to Rosie and said very quietly, "Those fellas are always talking about gettin' killed. I wish they wouldn't do that."

"It could happen."

Then Drake grinned at him. "Course, *you* talk about dying all the time. Ever since I've known you, you've talked about your funeral and what sermon you wanted—and look at you! Why, you're strong as any man in the company."

"Aw, that's just the way it seems. I'm not a well man," Rosie lamented. He glanced at Drake. "You're not really worried, are you?"

"Me?" Drake shook his head sternly. "No, I'm not. But it seems like they are."

The fire crackled and sent sparks rising high toward the dark sky. Rosie watched them and then murmured, "Maybe they seen enough to know there's something to be scared of." He put his knapsack down for a pillow. "Probably won't sleep a wink tonight. My insomnia is giving me trouble again."

Then he promptly went to sleep, leaving Drake to stare into the fire and think of the coming battle.

The next day began, it appeared to Drake, as one solid, unbroken crash of thunder. At early dawn he woke up with a start to the roar of guns. Officers were screaming at the troops to form lines, and Lieutenant Smith's face was almost purple as he raged up and down.

Scrambling to his feet, Drake saw small flashes winking across the way. *Like the eyes of demons*, he thought. This, he knew, was Confederate fire, and his hands grew sweaty as he checked his weapon.

"Form up! Form line of battle!" Lieutenant Smith yelled, and the sergeants moved around, getting their squads into position.

There was a moment of tense waiting, and then Jay Walters yelled, "There they come! There they come!"

Drake looked across the broken field. He caught fleeting glimpses of men darting from tree to tree and dropping to the ground to reload.

This was not what he had expected. From the battle pictures he had seen, he expected lines of men in neat ranks to come across the field. Instead, the Confederates were screaming like demons, weaving and dodging, and it was almost impossible to get a bead on them.

Drake threw up his rifle and fired wildly, knowing that he would miss. His hands trembled as he pulled the muzzle upright and began to reload. He had no sooner reloaded than the man beside him gave a cry and fell, clutching his leg. Blood stained the ground.

At once Royal Carter was there, tying a tourniquet around the leg and saying, "You'll be all right, soldier. We won't leave you!" Then he jumped up and looked down the line. "You're shooting high! You're shooting uphill! Aim low—for their legs."

Bullets and minié balls hummed through the air, one of them so close to Drake's ear that it sounded like an angry bee. He flinched involuntarily. Then he leveled his musket and tried to catch a clear target, but black gun smoke cast a dense fog over the battlefield, making it almost impossible to see. Blindly he pulled the trigger, reloaded, fired. He was like a man building a box, who stubbornly performed the routine actions necessary. He rammed powder into the musket, thrust the wad in on top, then the bullet, then another wad, then the percussion cap, and then he would level the rifle and fire.

"Charge! Charge!" The call went up and down the line. "Get ready for the charge!"

Rosie was beside Drake, his lips black with powder from the cartridges. "Pretty hard work, ain't it, Drake? Put your bayonet on. Didn't you hear the lieutenant? We're going to have a bayonet charge."

Drake gaped at him as if he hadn't understood, then he nodded. With fumbling hands he attached his bayonet and waited.

"Charge! Charge!"

Up and down the line, the Washington Blues lunged forward. Drake's legs felt numb. It took a force of will for him to move. He could not understand what was happening to him. Then he saw he was falling behind, and he tried to hurry. Rosie was already thirty yards ahead, yelling and screaming. He saw Royal turn and look back at him, and somehow this made him angry.

What's the matter with me? he thought wildly. *Come on, Bedford. Let's go!*

Stumbling forward into the smoke, Drake saw members of his company go down. Some dropped without a sound. Others screamed and clutched at their faces, at their throats, at their stomachs.

And then suddenly out of the smoke appeared a huge man holding a bayonet before him. He was Confederate, but his uniform was simply butternut pants and checkered shirt and a slouch hat. He had thick blond whiskers, and his lips were drawn back, exposing yellowish teeth. He was screeching at the top of his voice—but all that Drake focused on was the razor-edged bayonet.

He had no time to throw up his own weapon, for the enemy was on him. He saw the bayonet plunge toward him, and he suddenly lost all ability to move. Then, abruptly, the Confederate, with a look of surprise on his face, pitched forward, hit the ground, and lay still at Drake's feet. His musket tumbled away.

"Come on, Drake! Let's go! You all right?" Royal grabbed his arm. "We've got them on the run!"

Drake whispered, "All right, all right. I'm coming." Gripping his weapon, he stumbled ahead.

Royal moved away, encouraging other members of the squad. The Confederates were falling back, and there was a wild cry of victory from Company A as they charged.

And then, unexpectedly, there was a surprise attack from the right side. Some Confederates had apparently hidden in a grove of trees, and now they stormed out, tearing through the Blues with a terrible barrage.

Drake stared at the falling men. He heard the Confederates screaming, and the bores of their muskets seemed as large as the mouths of cannons. Something touched his side. He looked down to see that a bullet had neatly slit his uniform.

Suddenly Drake knew that there was no hope. Bullets were ripping the air beside him; it would be suicide to stay. Without thought, he dropped his musket, whirled, and began to run. His one desire was to get away from that terrible fire before he, too, was killed.

He heard a voice crying, "Drake! Drake, don't run!" He ignored it, however, and ran even faster.

Other men were approaching in thin ranks— their support troops. They asked, "What is it? What's going on?" but Drake did not answer. Blind fear took hold of him, and he ran and ran and ran.

9
A Defeated Army

No one ever knew the exact roll call of heroes at the Battle of Chickamauga. It was a fierce battle with great courage shown by both Confederate and Union soldiers. The dead and wounded lay across the fields, and both sides suffered dreadfully.

One man became famous as a result of this battle. Before he was ten years old, Johnny Clem had run away from his home in Ohio to be a drummer boy. But at Chickamauga, he armed himself with a sawed-off musket and shot and wounded a Confederate officer.

After the war he was appointed a second lieutenant. When he retired at the age of sixty-five, he was a major general. Johnny Clem was the last man active in the armed forces who had actually fought in the Civil War.

When the battle was over, the Union army began its retreat back toward Chattanooga.

The Southern general, Bragg, spoke with a Confederate soldier who had been captured and then escaped. The soldier, who had seen the Federals for himself, said to the general, "They're retreatin', General."

But Bragg would not accept the man's story. "Do you know what a retreat looks like?" he asked.

The soldier stared back at him and replied, "I ought to, General—I been with you during the whole campaign!"

Bragg decided not to continue the fight. His army was completely worn down. When the count was in, it would reveal that Confederate casualties had been greater than those suffered by the North. The Confederates lost 18,000 men—killed or wounded or captured—while the Federals lost approximately 16,000.

General Bragg had also lost a third of his artillery forces. When someone pressed him to pursue the fleeing Union troops, he protested that he couldn't because his wagon trains did not have sufficient horses and his artillery was almost completely bereft of the animals that pulled them.

By September 22, the entire Federal army was safely inside its Chattanooga defenses, and General Rosecrans put his men to shoring up the fortifications.

General Bragg moved the Southern troops up to the outskirts of Chattanooga and decided to starve Rosecrans into submission.

"We've got him where we want him!" he said confidently. "His destruction is only a matter of time."

"Hey, Professor, did you hear about Drake?"

Royal dropped his shovelful of dirt and looked up at Rosie, who had appeared at the top of the ditch. Royal's hands were blistered, and he laid the shovel down and flexed them, grunting with pain. "No, what about him?"

Rosie had somehow managed to avoid most of the work of building defenses. He turned up, of course, at sick call every day. But now, as he stood looking down at the ditchdiggers, he seemed in good health to Royal.

"What did he do now?" Royal asked in disgust.

"Another fight. Some fella made a remark about the way he run off, and Drake just peeled his potato." Rosie cast his light blue eyes up at the sky in an expression of awe. "He was a great big fella too. Done some prizefighting. Drake cut him down to size all right."

Walter Beddows, beside Royal in the ditch, asked, "How did he get in trouble over that?"

"Major Bates was passing by." Major Bates was the commander of the Washington Blues and was strict concerning fighting in the ranks. "He hauled Drake up and gave him a dressing down. I reckon he's gonna pull guard duty for quite a spell to make up for that."

"Where is he now?" Royal asked.

"Last I seen, Sergeant Pickens was takin' up where the major left off. Ira sure don't like it when any of his squad gets in trouble." Rosie wagged his head sadly. "Don't see why Drake has to be so put out about everything."

Royal answered quickly, "I think he's still ashamed of running away. You know how Drake is—he's awful proud."

"Well, he wasn't the only one who run off," Rosie protested. "I seen lots of fellas who got kinda *confused* about where the front line was in that there fight. Matter of fact, I might of run off myself with just a little more encouragement from them Rebels."

"Drake's just got to face up to it," Beddows put in. "I guess he never run from anything before, did he, Rosie?"

"Not Drake Bedford. He always took a lot of pride in bein' the toughest fella around, and now when he looks like a weakling—why, it just sort of humiliated him."

The three men stood talking idly for a time. They were all sick and tired of digging and building fortifications, and saw little sense to it. The two armies lay face-to-face, so close the Yankees could hear the Confederate signals. Rebel tents dotted the hillsides. They could see Rebel signal lights on the summit of Lookout Mountain and up on the knob of Missionary Ridge.

Royal glanced across to where the Confederates were camped. "We'll likely have another big fight on our hands. Those Rebels look pretty strong!" he observed.

At that moment Drake stalked up. His handsome face was flushed, and his lips were drawn tight. Anger, Royal saw, was bottled up inside of him, and it would take only a word to set him off again.

"Hello, Drake," he said cheerfully enough. "Come to give us a hand with this blasted ditch?"

Drake passed him a sullen look and jumped down into the trench. Without a word he picked up a shovel, and soon the dirt was flying.

Walter Beddows exchanged a glance with Royal and said, "Don't work so hard, Drake. Leave a little of this here dirt for Royal and me."

Drake turned to him and said shortly, "You tend to your diggin', Walter, and I'll take care of mine." He had actually done very little work on the fortifications, but now he was just ill-tempered enough to throw himself into it.

"Well," Royal said quickly, "maybe we'll get to go into town when we get this ditch dug. I asked

Sergeant Pickens, and he said we might get a shot at it."

This excited some other soldiers, sweating as they went by, but Drake made no response whatsoever.

Later on Rosie tried to talk with Drake.

The company was lodged in a large, barnlike abandoned factory, and Drake was lying on his cot, staring up at the ceiling.

Rosie sat down on his own cot and rubbed his legs. "You know, I got these shootin' pains in my legs. Maybe I better go see the surgeon again." Then he stared at his legs with dismay. "Sure hope they don't have to come off. I heard about a fella once who got shootin' pains, and they had to take off one of his legs."

Drake turned his head to the side, his mouth pulled down in a frown. "There's nothing wrong with your legs, Rosie," he said shortly. He was obviously still seething over the dressing down the major had given him. "And if Ira Pickens says one more word to me, I'm gonna bust him!"

"No, sir, you don't want to do that, Drake!" Rosie protested, forgetting his ailments. Alarm was in his voice. "Don't ever hit nobody that's over you, not an officer or not even a sergeant."

"I don't care what happens," Drake said sullenly. He closed his eyes as if that would shut out Rosie's words.

Rosie continued to argue for some time but found himself completely ignored. "Well," he said, "I guess I'll lie down here myself and rest awhile. A man in my condition needs lots of rest."

The next day Rosie and the rest of the squad were working again on the ditch when Sgt. Ira Pickens came by.

"You fellas keep at it," he said. "Those Rebels over there may decide to pay us a call."

"Aw, they're as fought out as we are, Sarge," Walter Beddows said. He tossed a small shovelful of dirt up on the edge of the ditch and grinned. "Why don't you come down here and help us?"

Ira Pickens was a veteran by this time, though he was very young. He'd turned into a fine sergeant. "They didn't make me sergeant to dig ditches," he remarked. "Just to stay on the backs of you lowly privates. Now you get with it, Walter. Someday you'll be a sergeant like me."

Rosie watched Ira walk along a few steps and glance at Drake, who was leaning against the raw earth of the bank, staring down at his feet.

"Won't do no good to study that dirt, Drake," Ira said. "Start pitching it up here."

Rosie suspected that Drake had slept little during the previous night. By now most men would have gotten over a bawling out from an officer, but not Drake Bedford. He glared up at Ira and said abruptly, "Dig all the dirt you want, Pickens. Just don't be telling me what to do!"

Ira looked taken aback. His eyes narrowed, and he said, "Get to work, Drake. Don't give me any of your back talk."

Drake laughed harshly. Then he cursed the sergeant and ended up by saying, "You're not gonna tell me what to do."

"How'd you like a little trip to the guardhouse?" Ira inquired. He was a peaceful young man, but he could not ignore this sort of behavior from his men.

"Now get to work, Drake, or that's where you'll wind up."

Drake threw down his shovel and was on the lip of the ditch in one swift movement. To Rosie's horror, he lashed out and struck the sergeant in the face.

Pickens was knocked backward, and blood began to flow from his nose.

Drake stood over him saying, "I'll do what I please, Pickens."

Rosie and Royal bounded up out of the ditch. Each took one of Drake's arms, and Rosie said, "Now you done it!" He groaned, holding on tightly. "Now, you tell Ira you're sorry there, and maybe you'll get out of this."

"That's right, Drake," Royal agreed.

Blood from the sergeant's nose had stained his uniform, and anger was in his eyes. He got to his feet. "Bring him along. We'll see if a stay in the guardhouse will make him a little bit more easy to live with."

But Drake refused to go to the guardhouse, and finally Ira had to summon others from the company to manhandle him.

Then Lieutenant Smith was called in, and he scowled, saying, "You're not much of a fighting man when it counts, Bedford. Why didn't you show a little of this when we were facing the Rebels?"

Drake looked him straight in the eye and called him a vile name.

Lieutenant Smith's face flushed. "Throw him in the guardhouse! Let's see how a few days on bread and water will satisfy him."

Rosie talked to Royal later. "Well, it looks like Drake's done tore it now," he said sadly. He shook

91

his head and added mournfully, "He's gonna hate that place. I spent one day in it once for not saluting an officer, and I was ready to quit a long time before they was. It's a bad place."

"Maybe it'll teach Drake to be a little bit more polite."

Rosie shook his head. "No, I don't reckon it will. He's so mule-headed stubborn that I don't think anything could do that."

Lori opened the door and smiled. "Why, Royal," she said, "come in—I really didn't expect to see you."

Royal had managed to get permission from Lieutenant Smith to spend an afternoon in town. He had carefully shaved and dressed in a clean uniform and found his way to the Jenkins home, a two-story, white frame house on the outskirts of Chattanooga.

He entered and looked around. "Will it be all right with your parents if I come calling?"

"Of course it will," Lori said. "They're not in right now, but they'll be back soon."

She was wearing a white dress that fitted her neatly, and her auburn hair was done up in a fashion that Royal had never seen before. The sunlight came through the windows just then, striking it, and it gave off red glints. "You look so good, Lori," he said simply.

Lori flushed at his compliment. "Why, thank you, Royal. Come into the kitchen. I was making a batch of cookies."

Royal followed her and sat on a high stool, watching as she worked. When she asked about Drake, he sighed. "It's not good news, Lori. He got

92

into a fight with a sergeant and got put in the guardhouse."

"What was the fight about?"

Royal did not want to tell the entire story and said simply, "Oh, you know Drake. He's just hot-headed."

"Will he have to stay there long?"

Shifting uncomfortably on the stool, Royal ran his hand through his crisp blond hair. "Not too long, I hope. Sergeant Pickens is a good man. He's the one that Drake had the fight with. The sergeant went to the lieutenant and said it wasn't all Drake's fault. I expect maybe he'll be getting out in maybe a week."

"I hate to hear that happened," Lori said. She cut perfect circles in the cookie dough with a tin can while she kept Royal talking about the battle and what he had been doing. Then she popped a pan of cookies into the oven and took off her apron. "Now, I'll fix some coffee—or would you rather have tea?"

"Coffee's fine," Royal said. "When will the cookies be done?"

Lori looked very pretty as she stood there laughing at him. "In ten minutes or so. You're always interested in sweets, aren't you?"

"Yes, I am." Suddenly Royal took her hand. It still had flour on it. "I always did like sweet things."

Again Lori blushed but quickly laughed again. "You soldiers are all alike!" she exclaimed. "Always telling lies to young ladies."

"And I bet you've heard a lot of 'em, with all the soldiers in town."

Lori did not answer, but she drew her hand back. "You behave yourself." She made coffee and,

93

when the cookies were done, laughed to see how greedily he gobbled them up.

"Don't strangle yourself!" she admonished. "You can have all you want."

"Can I have some to take back to camp?"

"Yes, you can, and be sure you take some to Drake."

"I'll do that!" Royal promised.

They talked for more than an hour, and then Lori's parents came in. Micah Jenkins was a tall man of forty-five. Her mother was younger. They both welcomed Royal.

"Can you stay for supper, Private?" Mrs. Jenkins asked.

"Well, I think I can. I'll have to get back before midnight, though."

Mr. Jenkins chuckled. "We don't usually eat until midnight, soldier, but we'll fill you up and get you back in plenty of time."

Royal thought the evening was wonderful. Mrs. Jenkins was an excellent cook, and her daughter was almost as good. When they finally sat down, the table was piled high with fried chicken, mashed potatoes, green beans, and onions. When that was gone, Royal applied himself to the cherry pie that Lori had made for him.

Pushing his chair back, he said with satisfaction, "I wish you'd sign on as our company cook, Mrs. Jenkins. We don't get cookin' like this."

"I don't expect any army food is like this," Mr. Jenkins agreed.

Then Lori's father leaned back in his chair and encouraged Royal to talk about himself. Soon the Jenkinses knew a great deal about the Carter family back in Kentucky.

When it was time to go, Royal shook Mr. Jenkins's hand and said fervently, "I sure appreciate your hospitality, sir."

"Come back any time you can, Royal." Mr. Jenkins put his arm around his wife, saying, "We can always find a meal for a good soldier, can't we, Tillie?"

"We sure can—and next time bring some of your friends with you."

The two disappeared then, leaving the young people alone.

"This has been great for me," Royal said. "You have wonderful parents, Lori."

"They liked you too. I could tell."

The air was cool on the porch, but they stood talking for ten minutes. Finally Royal said, "Well, I've got to go now, Lori."

She held out her hand, and he took it. "It's been so good to see you. Come back as often as you can."

All the way back to camp, Royal's heart was high. Then he endured some teasing from the rest of the squad—until he passed out the cookies and the remains of the cherry pie.

After a week, Drake was released from the guardhouse. When he came into the barracks, Royal could see that imprisonment had not improved his temper. But all the squad greeted him warmly, and Rosie said, "Glad you're back, Drake. Wasn't too bad, was it?"

Drake sat down on his bunk and glared at the rest of the squad.

He probably feels humiliated, Royal thought—*perhaps even wants to apologize to Pickens, but that would mean backing down.*

Drake said, "What's been going on around here since I been in the pokey?"

"Well," Rosie said, "we been gettin' lots of pies and cakes."

"Yea!" Jay Walters agreed. He grinned at Royal. "Royal's sweetheart there—she lives in Chattanooga. She's been cookin' up just for us. All kinds of good stuff."

"That Miss Jenkins is sure a fine cook," Walter said.

Drake shot a glance at Royal but said nothing. Later on he did inquire, "So you found Lori, Royal?"

"Yes, her folks live on the edge of town. We'll go over there as soon as we can get permission from the lieutenant. They want you to come too."

Suspicion touched Drake's eyes. "I guess you been telling them how I ran away."

Royal shook his head. "Haven't said a word. That's all over, Drake. Why don't you just forget it?"

But he was sure Drake could not forget it.

Five days later Royal and Drake did manage to wrangle passes—mostly through the agency of Sgt. Pickens. As the two of them made their way to town, Drake appeared more like himself. "Well, Royal, pretty nice of the sergeant to put in a word for me. He's not one to hold a grudge, I'll say that for him."

"No, Ira's a good sergeant."

Drake was warmly welcomed by the Jenkins family, and the meal was, as usual, very fine. Lori seemed especially glad to see Drake, and Royal saw to it that he spent some time playing checkers with Mr. Jenkins so that Drake and Lori had opportunity to visit alone.

They got back to the barracks on time, and Rosie said, "Did you bring us any goodies?"

"Sure did." And Royal produced the cake that Lori and her mother had prepared.

Walter Beddows said, "Here's a letter come for you, Royal."

Royal took the letter from him and, while the squad was enjoying their cake, he opened it.

Walter Beddows glanced up at Royal's face. "What's the matter, Royal? Bad news?"

"Some kind of sickness going around home. Sarah's real bad," he said slowly.

Jay Walters, who had enlisted at the same time as Royal, said, "I got a letter from my folks about that. Lots of people got it. Smallpox, I think."

The news dampened Royal's spirits, and he found it hard to join in his friends' light talk. Later that night, when he and Jay talked about it, he said quietly, "I'm real worried about Sarah, Jay."

"She'll be all right."

"Not sure about that. A lot of folks are sick, and I'd hate to see anything happen to her."

Royal went to bed, saying a special prayer for his sister. He thought about the others at home. Pineville seemed so far away from Chattanooga, and he wished he could be back there to help.

Finally he prayed, "Well, Lord, You'll just have to take care of the folks there. I know You can, and I'm asking You to do it."

10

"You Mean—She Might Die?"

A dull September sun threw feeble gleams down through a bank of white-gray clouds. Ezra Payne, who had been weeding the garden, looked up and frowned. Then he turned to his companion. "Leah, it looks to me like we are gonna get some rain."

Leah was wearing a pair of Royal's ancient overalls, bleached almost white from many washings. She straightened and glanced at the sky. "I hope it doesn't rain like it did last month. We needed it then, but we don't now."

Ezra smiled down at her, admiration in his eyes. "That was a toad strangler, wasn't it?" Then he pulled another weed, studied it thoughtfully, tossed it aside. Looking back at Leah, he said, "You're worried about Sarah, aren't you?"

"Of course I am!"

Leah's tone was short, and Ezra said quickly, "That was a dumb question. Of course you're worried. We all are."

"If there was just something we could *do!*" Frustration swept across Leah's face, and she kicked at a large cucumber. It had grown too big to make good eating, and now it split in two. The broken halves went skidding across the dark ground. "There's not anything anyone can do—even the doctor."

"She seemed a little bit better this morning, I thought. At least that's what your ma said."

"I wish they'd let me go in and see her," Leah muttered.

"But you might catch it too. I wouldn't want to see that happen."

"Ma is worn out with taking care of her. I've tried to look after the house as well as I can, but I want to see Sarah."

"I expect your ma knows best. Too bad your pa's gone on one of his trips to the army. You reckon he's heard of the sickness by now?"

"I doubt it. You know how slow the mail is with the war and all."

They worked their way down the long rows, gathering the late harvest. Soon Leah's bag was filled with squash, cucumbers, and okra. "We've got enough here—let's go to the house, Ezra."

"All right. I guess we got plenty."

Soon they were sitting at the table on the back porch, cleaning and trimming vegetables.

Ezra held up a long piece of okra. "I sure do like fried okra," he said. "Nothin's much better than that to me." He saw, however, that Leah's mind was elsewhere. Feeling rather helpless, he said, "I guess it's a good thing the Tollivers were able to keep Esther and Morena. Sure wouldn't want them to get sick."

"Yes, it was nice of them." Leah's voice was short.

The dreaded smallpox had swept through the community. Whole families came down with it, and the doctors knew little to do.

"I'm going to get that new kind of medicine that keeps you from getting smallpox. If Sarah'd had it done before, she wouldn't be sick now."

"I don't know . . ." Ezra shook his head doubtfully. "The way they explained it to me, they scratch your arm and put in some blood from a cow or a horse that's been infected with smallpox. That doesn't sound smart to me—giving you the disease!"

"The way it works," Leah explained—she trimmed a cucumber and tossed it into the bucket —"you get just a little bit of smallpox, and then you can never have it again."

"I guess so, but it sure sounds odd."

Ezra and Leah had just carried the vegetables into the kitchen when a thumping sound came from outside. They looked up as Tom shoved the door open with a shoulder and swung himself in. His crutches thudded on the floor, and he held his maimed leg high.

Tom had taken Sarah's sickness hard—harder than any of them would have imagined. When her illness had been diagnosed as smallpox, he had still insisted on visiting in her room. "I've already had smallpox," he said. "Can't hurt me." From then on, he had spent time with Sarah every day.

In one hand Tom held a collection of wild flowers. Looking rather sheepish, he said, "I found these out in the field. I thought Sarah might like them."

"Oh, they're beautiful! Let me put them in a vase." Leah jumped up and located a green vase that her mother had gotten as a wedding present years ago. She put water in it, arranged the flowers neatly, then extended the vase to Tom.

"You can take them up to her," he muttered.

"I'll do no such thing!" Leah said indignantly. But then she smiled. "You picked them for her—so you can take them up. Go on, now."

"Well, all right."

Tom grasped the slender vase and managed to wrap his hand around the handle of the crutch at the same time. He thumped across the kitchen, and they heard him go down the hall, then up the stairs.

"He's getting along all right on those crutches," Ezra remarked.

"Yes, he is, and his wound is healing cleanly too. Dr. Brown said the surgeon did a good job."

Ezra glanced toward the door and lowered his voice. "I sure wish he'd let me make him one of those wooden legs. I bet I could do it."

Leah smiled at him. "I'll bet you could too, Ezra. You do everything so well along that line."

Her praise brought a flush of pleasure to his cheeks. "Well, it doesn't do much good," he declared finally, "if he won't let me make him one."

"Don't give up. Sooner or later, I know he's going to come to accept what's happened to him."

Upstairs, Tom stood before the door of Sarah's bedroom and knocked.

"Come in."

He opened the door and swung himself inside. The room was darkened, for it was a prevailing belief that sunlight would hurt the eyes of one afflicted with smallpox. Tom propelled himself across the room and squinted down at Sarah, lying in bed with the counterpane pulled over her. "Found these in the woods," he said. "Thought you might like them."

"Let me see." Sarah reached out a hand and took the vase. She raised her head and smelled the blossoms. "Thank you, Tom. I'll put them right here on the table."

Tom stood there awkwardly and at last said, "Can I get you anything?"

"Sit down and talk to me, that's all."

Tom lowered himself into a cane rocking chair

and placed his crutches on the floor. "How do you feel today?"

"Oh, I'm all right. I can't complain."

"You never do." Tom leaned forward and examined her features. "No breaking out yet," he said.

"No—not yet."

Something in her tone told Tom that she was worried. He thought he knew what the trouble was. "You're worried about getting scarred, aren't you, Sarah?"

"I guess I shouldn't be. I suppose I ought to be thankful just to survive."

"It's only natural that a pretty girl would worry about scars, but lots of people get by with just a little scarring. Sometimes even where it doesn't show. I never had any at all."

"Well, maybe I'll get mine right in the middle of my back." Sarah managed a weak smile.

She's feeling terrible, he thought. The fever had drained her of strength.

But now she attempted to show a little spirit and said, "Tell me what you've been doing, Tom."

"Why, nothing," he admitted. He looked down at his hands. "Picking flowers—that's about all I've done."

"Ma tells me you've been helping some with the work around the place. I think that's fine."

Tom looked up at her, pain in his eyes. "Not much a one-legged man can do on a farm."

Sarah said nothing for a moment. "I thank God every day that you didn't get killed. That was my greatest fear."

"Sometimes I wish—" Tom broke off and changed the subject. "I got a letter from Pa this morning. He and Jeff are all right. Not in any fighting right now. Things are pretty bad there in Richmond though—and in all the South."

"How does your father talk—I mean about the war?"

Tom leaned back in the chair and brushed his hair out of his eyes. "He doesn't say much, but I can tell what he thinks."

"What's that?"

"He doesn't think there's much hope the South will ever win. I guess that's what I think too." He thought back over the last battles—at Gettysburg, at Chattanooga, where the South had suffered tremendous loss of life. "Can't go on forever," he said quietly. "Sooner or later it'll have to be over. If the North loses fifty thousand men, Lincoln just issues a call, and then there are fifty thousand more. But when the South loses fifty thousand men, the ranks just get that much thinner. Only one end to that."

"I suppose you'll be very sad if that happens."

Tom closed his eyes. "I don't know, Sarah. I would have at one time. But now, I just don't know." He changed the subject again. "Jeff's all right. He misses this place. Leah especially."

They talked until finally Sarah drifted off to sleep. Tom sat beside her for a long time. He had loved this girl for almost as long as he could remember. Now, looking at her still face, somewhat flushed with fever, he thought, *There never was a finer girl—not in the whole world! She deserves better than a cripple.*

He glanced down at his pinned-up trouser leg, and his lips drew thin. As quietly as he could, he picked up his crutches, put them under his arms, and swung himself to the door. He let himself out carefully, shut the door, and went downstairs.

There he met Mrs. Carter, who stepped out of the parlor and asked him, "How is she, Tom?"

"I don't know," Tom confessed. He balanced himself on one foot with the crutches under his arms. His brow furrowed. "What'll happen next? I was so young when I had smallpox . . ."

"We'll hope that she'll just begin to break out. Sometimes it goes bad, and people's fever goes so high they just can't tolerate it."

"You mean—she might die?"

Thoughtfully, Mrs. Carter gazed into Tom's face. Tom Majors had been in and out of her house all his life. Though he was grown now, she still saw traces of the small boy she had known. She saw that the war had worn him down, and the loss of his leg had made him sober. The cheerful good nature she had known was gone.

"Death is close to all of us, Tom," she said finally, "Closer than we know. It's not just in battles. You saw enough of that, but none of us know what will take us away. All we can do is trust."

Tom stared at her, then nodded briefly.

As he thumped away down the hall, Mary Carter thought, *He's grieving more than I thought was possible. I believe that Sarah's sickness has hit him as hard as losing his foot.*

She turned back into the parlor, glancing up at the tintypes on the wall—pictures of all the Carters and several pictures of the Majors family as well. She thought about old times before the war, when life had been so easy, and grief came over her. Her lips tightened, and she began cleaning the house with unnecessary vigor.

11

Love Never Changes

Leah looked up to see Pete Mangus coming down the road. As always, her heart beat a little faster when the mail came—which was not often. She thought, *Oh, I hope I get a letter from Jeff!* and held her breath to see if Pete would stop his Clementine at their gate.

When he did, her heart leaped. She jumped off the porch and ran out to meet him. "Hello, Pete. Do you have a letter for us?"

Pete Mangus grinned toothlessly at her. "You sure do look pretty, Leah," he said, sounding as if he had a mouth full of mush. He took in her light green dress, rather old and faded but still looking nice. "You're sure growing up to be a pretty young lady. Wouldn't be surprised to get a wedding invitation from you one of these days."

Leah was accustomed to Pete's teasing and knew that he had to go through a certain amount of that before he delivered his mail. She endured it as patiently as she could, then finally interrupted. "Pete, *do* you have a letter for us?"

"Why, sure I do. Why else would I stop here?" the mailman demanded with surprise. He reached into his canvas bag, rummaged around, then brought out an envelope.

Holding it at arm's length, he squinted at the writing. "Yep, that's your letter, all right." He grinned at her and winked. "You're Miss Leah

Carter, I take it. Well, that's who this letter's addressed to."

Leah reached for it, her eyes shining, but he pulled it back, holding it away from her grasp. "Let's see—can't tell exactly who wrote this letter, but the handwriting looks familiar. Let me see now—"

"Oh, Pete, don't tease me," Leah begged. "Let me have the letter."

Mangus took pity on her and handed it over. "I was just funnin' you, Leah. It's from Jeff, though. I know his handwriting."

Leah snatched at the letter and walked quickly away.

"Hey," Pete yelped, "aren't you going to read it to me?" When she paid no attention to him, he kicked the mule's flanks. "Get up, Clementine! Gettin' so a fella can't get no gossip on this here mail route no more."

Leah sat down on the porch, holding her letter. She stared at her name, written in the full, open manner of Jeff's handwriting, and felt her heart beat faster. She did not get many letters. When one came from him, it was a high hour for her.

She delayed opening it, dreaming of what he would say. The last time, he had mentioned that she had pretty hair, and she had read and reread that letter until it was almost worn out.

Finally she could put it off no longer. Opening the envelope, she pulled the letter out and was disappointed to see that it was not very long—only a single sheet filled on both sides. She was surprised to see that it was written on an odd sort of paper.

"Why, this is *wallpaper!*" she exclaimed. Jeff had told her that paper was scarce in the South, and she smiled, briefly wondering if he had ripped the paper off the wall to have something to write on. Then she turned her attention to the letter itself:

Dear Leah,

You'll be surprised to get a letter written on wallpaper, but it was all I could find. Not a very pretty pattern either—but I didn't have any other choice. Sorry about that. Next time I'll try to find something better.

Pa and I are fine. The army is resting now, building itself up, as always happens after a big battle. That last battle at Gettysburg left us pretty lean. It's real sad to see all the empty cots. Fellows that I knew real well. Some of them never got back. Some of them were shot up pretty bad and have gone on home to be with their folks. At least they're out of the war.

I was sorry to hear in your last letter how poorly Tom was doing. We were lucky to get him back alive, but I sure never thought he would take losing his foot so bad. I wonder if it wouldn't be better for him to come back here to Virginia. Course, Pa and I will be pulling out almost any time, and he couldn't go with us. I wouldn't know where he would stay—unless it would be with your Uncle Silas. Makes me a little sad to think that we don't have a home anymore.

The food here is pretty lean. Prices have gone sky high in Richmond. It takes twenty dollars to buy a little old bit of flour you can almost stick in your eye! Everything else is high too. Blockade's gotten pretty bad, so nothing can come in. When a ship does come in, the docks are always lined, and people are there with all the money they can find, bidding on anything it brings.

The only news I have is that I went to a birthday party the day before yesterday. You remember Cecil Taylor? Well, it was his sixteenth birthday, and Lucy Driscoll brought me an invitation. Said that Cecil wouldn't hear but what I'd come to the party. I didn't have any kind of present, but Lucy begged so hard that I went anyway. I put on my new uniform that Pa bought me, polished up my boots, and off we went.

Lucy has changed a lot. It seems like she's growing up real quick. She had on some kind of a rose-colored dress with embroidery all over it, and she'd fixed her hair some new way that I never saw before. Sure did look pretty.

When we got to the party, it was real nice. They had some musicians there, and it was kind of a dance and a birthday party combined. Everybody asked about you, and I could tell that they wished you were here. So do I! Lucy said to tell you "Hello." We didn't get back until real late, but we sure had a good time.

Well, keep on doing the best you can for Tom. I'm praying that he'll get his mind straight over this thing. We sure appreciate all you folks have done for us. Give Esther a big kiss for me.

By the way, Lucy's dress wasn't as pretty as the one you wore at our last birthday party—and Lucy's not as pretty as you are, either!

With warm regards,
Jeff Majors

Leah exclaimed angrily when she read that Jeff had gone with Lucy to a party, but then she read the last few lines over and over, her cheeks glowing.

She was startled when a voice said, "Get another letter, Leah?"

Leah turned around to see Ezra passing by. "Why, yes—it's from Jeff."

"He all right?"

"Yes, the army's not fighting right now."

"I guess he's wondering about Tom." Ezra looked solemn. "I wish Tom could see his brother and his pa. Maybe they could talk some sense into him."

"That doesn't sound very likely," Leah said.

"What else did Jeff say?"

"He said that . . . well . . . he said I was prettier than Lucy Driscoll."

Ezra grinned at her. "I could've told you that."

"You don't know Lucy Driscoll."

"Sure don't—but you're prettier than she is."

It was the most extravagant compliment Ezra had ever paid Leah, and she laughed aloud. "You're getting to be quite a ladies' man—tossing those compliments around. Next thing, you'll be writing poetry."

"I don't reckon I'll do that," Ezra said ruefully. After they'd talked awhile longer, he said, "I guess you pretty much favor Jeff."

Leah looked up quickly and studied his face. "We been best friends for a long time, Ezra. We grew up together."

This seemed to trouble him, but he said, "It's nice having a best friend." He got up and walked away.

Leah knew that Ezra fancied himself to be more or less in love with her. She liked him very much but wished that he didn't feel this way.

"I'll have to find a girl for him," she said. "He's such a nice boy." She thought for a minute. *Alice Simpson—I'll make sure that Alice sits next to him when we go to church Sunday. She's pretty, and she's got more sense than most girls. She'd be about right for Ezra.*

Tom Majors grew more despondent as Sarah's sickness continued. His appetite dropped off, and he was more silent than ever. Any attempts to bring him out of it were met with a rebuff, and he found himself sitting in his room for long periods, thinking of the past.

Something happened during this time that surprised him, however.

The Bible was not a new book to Tom, for he had been brought up in a Christian home, and he'd become a Christian at an early age. But since his wounding at Gettysburg, he'd become so bitter he had practically shut the door on the Bible and on church. He even refused to go to services with the Carters.

But one Sunday night after everyone else had gone to bed, he picked up the Bible that was lying on the dresser in his room. It was an old black Bible, worn limp. Inside the front cover was written "Daniel Carter. Born 1827. A gift from his father, Randolph Carter."

The yellow gleam of the lamp illuminated the page, and something about it caught Tom's attention. He had already undressed and was ready to lie down but was not sleepy. Propping his legs up on the bed and stuffing a pillow behind his back, he began turning the pages. He was interested to see small, handwritten dates by various verses. Sometimes the date had "Answered" printed beside it, sometimes not. Finally Tom figured out that the marked verses indicated God's promises. These, evidently, Dan Carter had claimed, and when an answer to prayer came, he had carefully dated it.

Thumbing through the Bible, Tom was amazed at how many answers were noted. He read for a long time, examining the verses and studying the dates. Evidently Mr. Carter had begun this practice as a young man.

Resting the Bible on his lap, Tom closed his eyes. He had always admired Dan Carter. No one in Pineville was more honest or devoted. Thinking back, he remembered how many kind words Dan Carter had had for him.

Why, when I was just a kid, knee high to a duck, he thought, *Mr. Carter always took me fishing with him when Pa couldn't go. He taught me how to ride a horse. He was always ready to pay attention to a small boy. I guess he's one of the best men I ever met.*

The lamp flickered, casting long shadows over the wall. The window was open, and a brisk breeze blew in, making the yellow flame dance. Silence filled the house except for the occasional groaning of timbers and the sighing of the wind—low, almost like a moan—as Tom continued to read in Dan Carter's Bible.

He came to the story of Joseph. Tom had always loved this story, and he realized that he had not read it in years.

He read about Joseph's being his father's favorite. He read about how his brothers hated him and threw him into a pit. Then they sold him into slavery, and he went off to a strange land.

Still, God was with him. Tom read more slowly as the story developed. Joseph found favor, first with his owner, then later with the jailer in the prison where he was thrown unjustly.

Tom paused and said aloud, "Pretty bad for a young boy to be thrown into a pit. Then sold into slavery. Then chucked into jail for something he didn't do."

He thought about that and began to read again. He traced the story of how Joseph was able to interpret the king's dream and become second in the land of Egypt. And of how, in the closing chapters of the book of Genesis, God used Joseph to rescue his family.

Tom's eyes grew misty. It was a moving story, and he threw his arm across his eyes.

Suddenly a strange feeling coursed through him. *Here I am,* he thought, *crying about losing a foot, when so many fellows are dead. Joseph here went through big problems too, but he never gave up on God!*

He tried to read again, but somehow he was terribly disturbed. He closed the Bible, turned off the lamp, lay back, and tried to sleep. In the darkness, thoughts kept coming at him. Finally, he sat up. He put his head in his hands and, for the first time since he had been wounded, began to pray.

"O God," he said—and his voice broke—"I've been acting like the world's awfulest baby. So many good men are dead, and here I am, crying like a whipped puppy because I had a little setback. God, I've been wrong about all this, and I've doubted You—and I'm sorry!"

112

The next morning, Sarah was sitting up in bed when Tom came to her door. Something in his face startled her. "Why, Tom! What is it?" she asked. "You look—strange."

He sat on the cane chair beside the bed and put down his crutches. "Sarah," he said abruptly, "I want to tell you something, but first I want to do something."

"What is it, Tom? What do you want to do?"

"This!"

To her amazement, he leaned forward and kissed her.

"Why—Tom!" she gasped.

"I've come to tell you that I love you, Sarah," he said. "I guess I nearly always have. I've told you enough times, but I wanted to tell you again."

Sarah reached out to him, and he took her small hand in his.

"I've been wrong, acting the way I have," he said.

"What's come over you, Tom?"

"I think it's the Lord. I was reading your father's Bible last night." His face grew stern. "I've been acting like a spoiled kid, and God took me to task for that. But it's all right—He's forgiven me. And now I want to ask you to forgive me for acting like such a baby."

"Why, of course, Tom. You don't have to ask that."

His eyes lit up. "That's what I wanted to hear," he said happily. "Now we're going back to where we were before. I remember what you told me in Gettysburg."

Sarah's smile disappeared. "That—that may not come, Tom," she said finally, her voice strained.

"You mean you don't love me anymore?"

"No, no, I don't mean that. It's just that . . ." Sarah struggled for words. Then she touched her face. "You know what smallpox can do. I may be terribly scarred when this is over."

"I thought all this time you been telling me, Sarah," he said quietly, "that you loved me even though I lost my foot."

"Yes, that's true."

"But you think my love's not as strong as yours? That I wouldn't love you if you had a scar? That's not fair, Sarah. My faith's been pretty weak, but all the time I've known that I love you."

Sarah's face glowed. She said, "That's sweet of you, Tom, but we'll have to wait and see how bad it will be."

"I don't care *how* bad it is. We're going to believe God. We're going to take whatever He gives us. I want you to hurry up and get well."

There was excitement in his voice, and she could see it in his eyes. It was so good to see him excited about something after the past terrible weeks. "I'll do the best I can, Tom, but—"

He touched her cheek. "You just hurry up and get well," he said, "because as soon as you do, I'm gonna have a surprise for you."

"What is it?"

He laughed quietly. "It wouldn't be a surprise if you knew, would it? You just get ready. You get well, and I'll take care of the surprise!"

12
Lori and Drake

Anyone interested in the behavior of spoiled children might read the history of the Union and Confederate generals following the Battle of Chickamauga.

General Rosecrans, the Federal general, threw a temper tantrum. He removed some of his officers who had been in the battle, and those he could not remove he demoted. What he did not realize was that President Lincoln was furious with *him* for not winning the battle.

The Southern general, Bragg, spent a great deal of time trying to find officers to blame, and he removed most of *them*. He made one serious mistake, however—he relocated the largest part of General Nathan Bedford Forrest's cavalry.

General Forrest marched into Bragg's tent and called him a scoundrel and a coward. Everyone within half a mile heard Forrest say, "You may as well not issue any more orders to me, for I will not obey them. If you ever again try to interfere with me or cross my path, it will be at the peril of your life!"

General Bragg had a hot temper himself, but he well knew that General Forrest had killed more of the enemy personally than any other general on either side. He said no more to General Forrest.

The two armies lay face-to-face, neither able to move.

The Federals had to get their supplies from Nashville. Part of the trip was by wagon train over a steep, winding trail scarcely more than a footpath. Then the wagons had to cross into town over a pontoon bridge. The trip took from eight to twenty days—and under the heavy rains that followed the Battle of Chickamauga, the mules had to struggle through belly-deep mud.

The siege wore on. It became more and more difficult to feed the animals. Half-starved, the mules chewed on trees, fences, wagons, and anything else they could reach. More than ten thousand of them died.

Food in Chattanooga grew so scarce that men stole corn from the horses. They hunted for it on the ground where the animals had been fed. By mid-October, soldiers were assailing their officers with cries of "Crackers!" The men were now eager to see the usually despised hardtack.

A newspaperman—George Shanks, of the *New York Herald*—wrote, "I have often seen hundreds of soldiers following behind the wagon trains which had just arrived, picking out of the mud the crumbs of bread, coffee, rice, and so forth, which were wasted from the boxes and stacks by the rattling of the wagons over the stones."

But the townspeople suffered most of all. While the army made some effort to feed its men, the non-combatants had no one to feed them. Many had their houses torn down to provide fuel for campfires. Most of the civilians eventually fled from the city.

Some of this was on Drake's mind as he got to his feet and walked away from his squad. The situation had been worse for him than for the others. They were suffering only the misery of poor food and bad weather—he was suffering even more from the torment of guilt.

After running away in battle, he knew the rest of the company looked on him as a coward. Even more difficult was the fact that he knew he *was* one. As the weeks wore on, his self-disgust had festered until he now little resembled the cheerful, happy-go-lucky young man who had joined the army.

Drake walked along, drawing his thin coat around him to cut off the cold breeze. His thoughts went again to Lori Jenkins. *She must despise me,* he thought bitterly. *What girl wouldn't despise a fellow that would run away? And she's right.*

Looking overhead, he saw dark clouds gathering and thought that snow was in them. This depressed him also, for he hated cold weather. He longed to be back in Pineville, to be out of the army, but he knew he couldn't turn the clock back. For more than an hour he walked his solitary way, berating himself.

Early the next morning, however, Drake was approached by Ira Pickens. "Bedford, I don't know why, but you're gonna get a pass to go into town. You better go take it before the lieutenant changes his mind."

With surprise in his eyes, Bedford stared at the sergeant. "They run out of real soldiers to give passes to?" He turned away.

"Wait a minute." Pickens followed him.

Ira was a good sergeant. Drake knew that. Now it looked as if Pickens was going to try once more to set him straight.

"Look, Drake," he said, "you made a mistake. Well, we all make them. You think you're the only man that ever ran away when he heard a shot fired? I was at Bull Run, and I don't mind telling you I ran like a rabbit! All of us did, but most of us managed to swallow that and get on with the war. . . ."

Sergeant Pickens continued to speak earnestly to Drake, but soon apparently realized that his words were having little effect. "Well," he concluded, "go take your leave—but you're making a mistake, living in the past."

Drake did not thank Pickens, but he was glad for the unexpected leave. He cleaned up, shaved, and polished his boots. He caught a ride toward town with a supply wagon pulled by two skinny mules and soon found himself in front of the Jenkins house.

The wind was whipping out of the east, and he shivered as he dropped from the wagon.

The driver accepted his "Thanks for the ride" with a nod of his head and went on.

Drake crossed the yard and mounted the steps, but when he stood before the door he hesitated. The shame that was in him ran deep. He had the impulse to run, to leave without knocking. Having to face Lori while knowing his cowardice was painfully hard for him, but he pulled his shoulders back, set his jaw, and knocked.

When the door opened, Mrs. Jenkins exclaimed, "Why, Drake, come in the house!" She opened the door wide. "Let me have your hat. I'll go tell Lori you're here."

"Thank you, Mrs. Jenkins."

"You go on in the parlor now, and I'll fix some tea. That's always good on a chilly day like this."

"That would go mighty good, ma'am." Drake walked into the front room and stood staring at the family pictures on the wall. One of them he found particularly attractive. It was a picture of Lori when she was no more than five or six. She had on a frilly white dress with a full skirt, and her hair was fixed in curls that hung down her back. She wore a curious smile. He had told her when he first saw that picture, "You seem to have been planning some outrage."

She had replied, "I didn't want to have my picture taken, and Ma made me smile when I didn't want to."

Now, studying the photograph, he saw that even at that early age, Lori had traces of the beauty that was hers today.

He looked at the other pictures. The Jenkins family could trace its history far back. Drake wished he had had a steady family, but his mother died when he was young, and his father was a drinking man. Drake had been raised in a haphazard fashion, living in many places. Lately he had wondered what sort of a man he might be if he had been reared differently.

"Why, Drake, how nice to see you!"

He turned when he heard Lori's voice. She was wearing a dark blue dress that came to the top of her shoes, and a white sweater, and she looked very pretty.

"How long can you stay?"

"I've got an all-day pass."

"Oh, that's fine. Then we can have supper."

"It seems like I always come for supper," Drake said. "I wish I could take you out to a restaurant, but I'm broke. We haven't gotten paid in weeks. I guess Washington's forgotten about us."

"Oh, I can cook better than any old restaurant cook," Lori said. "But come sit down now and tell me what all you've been doing."

They sat on the horsehair sofa, and from time to time Drake added wood to the fireplace. The fire made a cheerful crackling noise, and when he poked it, sparks spiraled up the chimney. "Always liked a fire," he murmured, going back to sit beside her. He stared into the red and yellow tongues of flame that leaped and consumed the wood. "I used to want it to snow and be cold, just so we could build a fire—and then I hated the cold after it came."

Lori laughed quietly. "I'm the same say. I love to see it snow, but then I want it to be gone the next day."

Later on, Drake insisted on going out and cutting more firewood.

Mrs. Jenkins protested. But when he insisted, she said, "Well, put on some of my husband's old clothes—you can't spoil your uniform."

Drake was soon splitting red oak. It was a job that he didn't mind. The logs were approximately a foot and a half thick, and he sawed each into two short lengths with a bucksaw. When he had a pile, he stood them on end and with an ax split them into smaller chunks.

"You do that so well," Lori said. She had put on a heavy coat and a cap that covered her ears and a pair of woolen mittens. She sat on an upturned box and watched him.

"Not much to it," Drake said. He swung the ax over his head and hit one of the wood cylinders. It fell into two pieces, splinterless as a cloven rock.

"I've seen Daddy almost resort to profanity. He can't do this at all. Has to hire most of it done."

"I spent two years on a farm. I liked chopping wood better than anything." Drake thought back to the time when he had learned how to plow and how to milk, and he shared this with her.

"What are you going to do when the war's over? Be a farmer?" she asked.

"Don't know. Just trying to make it through," Drake said.

After he had finished chopping firewood, they went for a walk in the nearby woods. The wind was sharp, and dark clouds rolled overhead, but Drake's black mood disappeared for a while. Lori was so pretty and so cheerful that he found himself laughing as he had not since the incident of his cowardice.

When they returned to the house, Lori's father was there. "Well," he said, after greeting Drake, "it's time for us to see who's best at checkers."

"I thought we settled that last time, Mr. Jenkins." He had beaten the older man three games out of five. He grinned, saying, "I'd be glad to give you some lessons, though, if that's what you'd like."

"We'll see about that."

The two men played while Lori and her mother prepared supper.

When they were seated at the table, as usual Mr. Jenkins bowed his head and prayed a fervent prayer of thanksgiving. When he looked up from the prayer, he said, "The cupboard's a little bit lean, Drake. Food is pretty scarce around Chattanooga."

"This looks good to me," Drake said. There was a small platter of pork chops, a few potatoes, some canned tomatoes, and fresh bread. "I guess everybody is on pretty slim rations right now."

"Well, the Lord will provide," Mr. Jenkins said. "Help yourself."

They ate heartily what was there. Tonight there was no dessert. After the meal everyone went back into the parlor.

"Sing something for us, Drake," Mrs. Jenkins said. She sat herself down at the piano and ran her fingers over the keys. "You have such a beautiful voice. I love to hear you sing."

Drake grinned. "You wouldn't like some of the songs. I grew up pretty rough, Mrs. Jenkins. Learned a lot of songs I'd be better off not knowing."

"We don't have to hear those," she said. Mrs. Jenkins was a plump woman with a pretty face and lively brown eyes. "Do you know 'Lorena'?"

"I suppose every soldier in both armies knows that one."

"Lorena" was a sentimental tune that was sung around campfires. Just as soon as the army stopped and the campfires were made, you could hear this song floating in the air.

As the piano began to play, the parlor was filled with Drake's rich tenor.

After "Lorena," Mr. Jenkins said, "That's enough of the romantic stuff. That song makes you feel like you're stuck in molasses—too sweet for me. Let's have a lively tune, Drake."

"All right, you asked for it."

After Drake had sung several rollicking songs, they began to sing hymns. Drake knew some of them from the few church revival meetings he'd

122

attended—mostly looking for the attractive young ladies who were there.

Suddenly he saw tears in Mrs. Jenkins's eyes. *These hymns are real to her,* he thought. Glancing at Lori, he saw that she was affected by the hymn singing too. He felt strangely out of place and wondered if he would ever feel at home with godly people. It was a thought that had never occurred to him before.

Finally Mr. and Mrs. Jenkins tactfully left to "wash the dishes."

Lori and Drake sat before the fire again, and Drake grew unusually quiet.

Lori said, "You're not saying much, Drake. Is anything wrong?"

"I guess I don't have much to talk about. Nothing much happens in the army."

"Then tell me about your life when you were a boy."

Drake hesitated, then began to tell about his childhood. He had never done this before. He related his hard beginnings and the difficulties of his early years. He fixed his gaze on the fire and spoke quietly, his words punctuated by the popping of the flames as the log crackled.

When he finished, Lori said, "You've had a hard time, Drake."

"Better than some, though," he argued. "Up until this war came, I was doing fine."

Lori paused just a moment. "You're wasting your life, Drake. Do you know that? Everyone does who cuts God out."

He shifted uneasily, feeling her eyes riveted on him.

"I guess I haven't thought much about God at all," he admitted.

Then Lori began to tell how she had found the Lord Jesus and what He had meant to her life. He had known that she went to church, but this was a side of Lori that he had not seen. As Drake listened, he saw that she was sincere in her faith.

"I hate to see you waste your life," she said again. "Especially with the danger of battle before you."

Abruptly Drake turned to her. He said almost without thinking, "Lori, have you ever thought of me as a man you might marry some day?"

"Why, Drake—"

When she hesitated, Drake pulled himself together. "I guess not. I'm just not the sort of fellow you're looking for. I guess Royal's more along that line." He couldn't keep the bitterness out of his voice.

Lori said, "Drake, I'm not thinking about marriage at all right now—with Royal or with anyone else."

Glancing at her quickly, Drake saw that she was telling the truth, and that came as a relief. "I guess you're right. It's no time to think about permanent things. Everything is all up in the air. We might be in a big battle tomorrow."

He got to his feet. "I've got to get back. Can't tell you what it's meant to me, Lori—just getting away from camp for a while."

"I want to see you do well, Drake. I'll be praying that God will do something wonderful in your life. That you'll be safe and that your life will have meaning."

On his way back to camp, Drake reflected on her words. Bitterly he thought, *My life sure hasn't meant anything up to now. Just playing the fiddle at parties—what good does that do? A man ought to be more than a fiddle player!*

13
Prelude to Battle

During the siege of Chattanooga, many of the besiegers were as miserable as the besieged. Private Sam Watkins of the First Tennessee Regiment wrote about the miserable condition of the Confederate troops:

> Our rations were cooked up by a special detail ten miles in the rear, and were sent to us every three days; and then those three days' rations were generally eaten at one meal, and the soldiers had to starve the other two days and a half. The soldiers were almost naked, and covered all over with vermin and camp-itch, and filth and dirt. The men looked sick, hollow-eyed and heartbroken.
>
> Just when our provisions and hunger were at their worst we were ordered into the line. There we were reviewed by the Honorable Jefferson Davis. When he passed us with his great retinue of staff officers at a full gallop, he was greeted with the words "Send us something to eat, Jeff. I'm hungry! I'm hungry!"

September passed with both armies again simply waiting—and growing hungrier.

And then General Ulysses S. Grant was assigned to command Rosecrans's army. General Rosecrans quietly slipped away.

General Grant came to Tennessee, and the men saw at once that he was a different kind of general. When he arrived, the call sounded, "Turn out the guard for the commanding general!"

"Never mind the guard," Grant said, and the guard was dismissed.

Grant rode along the lines of battle, saluting men, and when his cavalcade passed by the Washington Blues, Rosie said, "He don't look like much, does he?"

Royal, standing beside Rosie, studied the small, nondescript figure of the new general. "He was tough enough to whip the Rebs at Vicksburg, so I reckon he'll do the same here in Tennessee."

Rosie continued to eye the general. "Had a dog once that looked kind of like him. He weren't worth much in the looks department, but he sure was a humdinger on a cold scent. You'd turn that hound loose, and he'd die before he'd quit." He studied Grant's bearded face. "I reckon that general there is just about like that old dog of mine."

That night, talk ran around the campfire about the campaign that was to come.

Ira Pickens remarked, "Seems like I've got to where I can smell a battle coming at us."

Grant had seen to it that the rations had improved, and Ira took a bite of the roast beef that had been issued. "I can't tell how bad it's going to be, but I think those Rebs are pretty stubborn over there."

Royal chewed thoughtfully, looking across the lines to where the Confederate army was settled into position on the high ridges. "I don't see how anybody can climb up Lookout Mountain to attack them. The Rebels got their guns aimed right down at us." He looked to his left. "And there up on Missionary Ridge, it's just about as bad. Pretty hard to fight a battle uphill, I'd say."

"Well, I don't reckon we'll try to go right up the hill," Ira said. "Maybe we'll try to flank 'em—get around one side or the other."

Drake sat back away from the fire, thinking as he ate. He had not made one remark about the military situation since he had run away.

As the men talked cheerfully, he thought again of Lori's words on his last visit. Most of the young men in his squad were Christians. One or two were hard cases, as in any army, but they were more Christian than most groups. Looking about at their faces, he thought, *If they get shot and killed in this battle, they'll be all right—if what the preachers say is true. I don't know about me, though. I guess there's not much hope for a fellow that's lived like I have.*

Soon after the meal was over, Walter Beddows piled some more wood on the fire, and the talk turned to religion.

"I heard a preacher say one time," Ira Pickens commented, "that any soldier got killed fighting for his country would go straight to heaven. What do you think of that, Professor?"

Every eye turned to Royal. He was the only one of the group who had attended college, and he was considered the final judge on matters where education was concerned.

"I'm no preacher—" he shrugged "—but I don't think that's true."

"Why, of course, it ain't true," Rosie piped up. "We're fighting for one side, and the Rebels are fighting for another side. We can't all go to heaven —*somebody's* on the wrong side."

Royal said quickly, "I don't think that's the point, Rosie. Men have fought in all kinds of wars all through history, but the Bible says it's not a matter of who we die for that settles that question." He hesitated. "The Bible says, 'You must be born again.' As long as we get that right, I know we're all right when we die."

One of the new members of the squad, a squat, bearded man named Tyrone Johnson, asked, "But what's that mean, Professor? I heard it all my life, but I still don't understand it."

"As I say, I'm no preacher, but I can tell you what that means," Royal said. "It means that all of us sin against God. Then when we die, we have to stand in judgment for our sins." He looked at the fire and then around at the faces highlighted by it. "But Jesus came so that we wouldn't have to face a God of judgment. On the cross He took all of our sins on Himself. That's why He died, Tyrone—so we could get forgiven and be what the Bible calls 'born again.'"

Tyrone clawed at his whiskers. "I don't see how that could be, though. Don't see how a man dying thousands of years ago has anything to do with me."

"I don't understand it all either," Royal admitted, "but I know the Bible says that when we believe in Jesus and call on God to forgive us, then somehow His blood washes us clean."

Tyrone's blue eyes glowed in the firelight. "I heard a song about that. Something about being 'washed in the blood of the Lamb.' Is that what that means, Professor?"

"That's what it means, Ty. When Jesus died, somehow He made it possible for us to get our sins forgiven. That's what I'm hangin' onto."

One by one several soldiers around the fire talked about where they stood. The squad had seen battle, but death in all of its ugly forms still lay before them, and most seemed well aware that they might soon be standing before God.

Drake took no part in the discussion, but the talk troubled him. It was all piling up—first, Lori's talking about his need of God, and now most of the squad seemed to be saying the same thing.

Later on, when many of the men had gone to bed, Rosie plumped himself down by Drake. "I don't think my liver is acting right," the lanky soldier complained.

"It didn't seem to hurt your appetite any." Drake smiled, amused again by his friend's many ailments. "You ate enough of that roast beef to supply the whole squad."

"Well, a man in my pitiful condition has to keep his strength up." Rosie held his side. "Somehow my liver don't feel right."

"I don't think your liver's *there*. I think that's your heart."

Rosie looked surprised. "Oh, then I'm having heart trouble instead of liver trouble. I have noticed lately that it's beating sort of irregular. Maybe I better go to the surgeon again."

"I don't think he can help you. Maybe you better eat some more supper."

"Aw, don't be making fun of my ailments, Drake."

The two sat in the firelight awhile longer. Finally Rosie shifted uneasily. "All this talk about gettin' saved—it kind of bothers me."

Drake looked over at his friend. "To tell the truth, Rosie, it makes me a little nervous too."

"You think it's right what the preachers say about heaven and hell?"

"I don't know. But it's bad news for us if they're telling the truth."

"Reckon *that's* the gospel." Rosie looked into the dying fire. The coals were almost golden. Picking up a stick he stirred them and watched the sparks fly upward. He looked beyond the sparks and said, "I reckon somebody made all them stars up there—they didn't make themselves. It makes you think, don't it?"

"Sure does." He saw that Rosie was truly troubled. "Maybe you better talk to one of those other fellas about gettin' saved."

Rosie shook his head. "Naw, I reckon that wouldn't be rightly fair to the Almighty."

"What do you mean by that?"

"I mean, it don't seem right. A fellow lives a pretty bad life, then—when it comes time maybe to end it all, like in this battle coming up—he goes running to God like a whipped puppy. Nope, I'll wait until it's all over—then I can meet God on a little better terms."

Somehow Drake felt this idea was wrong, but he had no answers. "We'll just have to see what it's like after we die, I guess. But these fellas—" he waved a hand toward their sleeping squad members "—they all seem so *sure* that they're going to heaven. Wouldn't be a bad thing to know you'd be all right, would it, Rosie?"

For once Rosie seemed to have forgotten his ailments. He sat hugging his knees, staring into the fire, and saying no more. But his face wore a worried expression. The two men had been friends for years. They knew each other's shortcomings. Drake was convinced that neither of them had any hope of heaven.

Now, as the guards called out faintly from the picket lines, the lonesome, mournful air about Rosie in turn made Drake feel almost desperate.

Still, there seemed nothing he could do. "Let's get to sleep," he said. "Maybe when we get through with this battle, we'll be able to go to church and find out about this religion thing."

The Jenkins house was packed almost to the walls. Soldiers from the Washington Blues were everywhere. Mr. Jenkins had decided to have Drake's whole squad in for a meal, and now, looking around, he wondered if he had gathered enough food for this hungry group.

His wife and Lori scurried around in the kitchen. They had scraped the bottom of the barrel to find enough food, but fortunately they had one pig left. Mr. Jenkins had slaughtered it just that afternoon, and now the whole house was rich with the odor of pork chops, sausage, and frying ham.

Then Mrs. Jenkins said, "Well, it's all ready. Let's get it on the table."

"I'll ask some of the men to help us," Lori said. She stepped into the parlor and said, "I need a little help setting the food on the table. Any volunteers?"

Instantly Rosie said, "I was a waiter once, Miss Lori." He grinned broadly, his homely face alight. "Let me help you."

"I'll help too," Royal spoke up. He pulled Drake to his feet. "Come on, Drake—let's earn our keep."

The three men went into the kitchen and, in a series of trips, loaded down the dining room table with platters of pork. Mrs. Jenkins had opened jars of home-canned vegetables, and soon the table was covered.

When all was ready, Mr. Jenkins said, "Now, let's get around this table, ask God to bless this food, and eat it."

The soldiers gathered around, some fifteen of them, and bowed their heads.

"It's good to have all of you young men here," Mr. Jenkins said. "I wish we could've had the whole regiment in, but this is as many as would fit." He bowed his head then and said, "O God, we thank You for this food. We thank You for these young men who have left their homes to serve their country. We thank You for their lives, and we ask that You draw every one of them to Yourself—that not one of them would go into battle unsaved. We ask this in Jesus' name."

"That was quite a sermon, Pa." Lori grinned at him and then smiled around at the soldiers. "My father always wanted to be a preacher, so he sneaks his sermons into his prayers."

"Never mind that," Mr. Jenkins cried out. "Grab a plate, fill it up, find a place, and then enjoy yourselves."

The young soldiers were not in the least adverse to this. Soon they were scattered throughout the house, wherever they could find chairs, with plates of food on their laps. Lori and her mother circulated with glasses of tea.

Finally Lori got herself a plate and looked for a spot to sit down. She saw a place between Drake and Royal and headed that way. "I'll sit here and listen to you two eat," she said.

Royal laughed aloud. "We don't get food like this very often."

"That's right, we don't, Lori," Drake said. "You and your mother are the best cooks I ever saw."

"Yes, my mother's a good cook. I've learned a few things from her."

"How does she make these pork chops so tender—and so juicy?" Drake asked.

"Well, it's fresh pork, for one thing, and she soaks them in a special sauce."

"Tastes better than any pork chop I ever had," Drake declared.

Across the room Rosie was talking to Mrs. Jenkins about his ailments.

"I guess I'll be able to get by another day on this fine meal," he said. Wagging his head sadly, he added, "My health's poorly, you know."

Mrs. Jenkins eyed the big, strapping young man, his face glowing with health. "I would never have guessed it, Rosie. What's your problem?"

Rosie chewed thoughtfully on his pork chop. "Well, I guess maybe I hurt more all over than I do in any specific place," he finally admitted. But then a grin crossed his lips. "But with pork chops like these I think I might make it through another day or two."

The talk around Lori and Drake and Royal rose happily.

Lori said, "It's nice to have your squad here."

"I expect we'll be moving out soon," Royal said. "It's good to have this meal together."

After supper, the soldiers attacked the dishes, insisting that Mrs. Jenkins and Lori not touch a plate. Sergeant Pickens oversaw the job. When every dish was spotless and stacked in the cabinets, the sergeant came back with his helpers, saying, "All set. Now let's have some music."

Mrs. Jenkins went to the piano, and soon old songs echoed through the house.

Ira organized a quartet, and they sang all the songs they knew, which was two. When the group finished, he said, "Drake, now let's have a song out of you."

Drake protested, but Lori whispered, "Go on. God's given you a voice—now use it."

Drake reluctantly sang several songs and then said, "Now that's enough solos. You all join in."

Before long, Sergeant Pickens said, "I've got to get these galoots home." He made a rather long speech, thanking the Jenkinses for their hospitality, then herded his men out.

Drake had time to say only a quick word to Lori. "This was a fine evening," he told her. "Thank you for having us all."

"I'm glad you could come, Drake." She smiled up at him. "I'll be praying for you. I know you've had a hard time, but God will be with you in the battle that is to come. I believe He's promised me that."

Drake gaped at her. "God's promised you that? What do you mean?"

"I know what's been bothering you, Drake. I've heard the stories."

"So they told you how I ran like a scared chicken?"

"You won't run anymore," Lori said, and her eyes were bright. "I just know in my heart. God has assured me that you will be a fine soldier."

Drake could think of no answer. "Good-bye," he said.

As they were marching back, Rosie asked, "What did Miss Lori say to you there on the porch?"

"She said—she said that no matter what I'd done in the past, I'd be a good soldier." He hesitated and added, "She said God told her that."

"Well, if Miss Lori says it, I believe it," Rosie said defiantly. He clapped Drake on the shoulder with his big hand. "Sometimes we sinners just have to go on the faith of the godly folks, so let's just believe what Miss Lori says."

Drake did not answer, but as they tramped along, thoughts flooded his mind. He finally said in his own heart, *I hope she's right. I sure need to be something different than what I am!*

14

Greater Love Has No Man

The battle that both Confederate and Union armies had waited for developed over three separate days.

On November 23 the first Union attack took place. It was called the Battle of Orchard Knob, and it had merely one purpose: General Grant was determined to learn whether or not the Confederates would retreat if attacked. Orchard Knob was only an outpost line in front of Missionary Ridge. The Federals captured it.

The Battle of Lookout Mountain, which took place on November 24, was to become famous because of its picturesque location and its poetic name, "The Battle Above the Clouds."

In fact, the battle was not fought at the top of the mountain above the clouds. It was fought in heavy mist on a wooded, rocky slope about five hundred feet below the crest. The rugged terrain and fog hampered both sides, but there was never any serious doubt as to the outcome. The Union forces outnumbered the Confederates at least six to one. The Rebels withdrew after dark to Missionary Ridge, and the next day the Stars and Stripes was planted on top of Lookout Mountain.

Sherman, the Northern general, would have to attack uphill to take Missionary Ridge. Furthermore, the hill was steep, difficult to climb, and defended by one of the finest divisions in the Confederate army. The Rebels were ready and waiting.

From early morning on the 25th until the middle of the afternoon, the Union troops kept up their assault on Missionary Ridge. The Rebels refused to retreat. In some places the ridge was so steep that the Confederate cannon could not shoot downhill, so they rolled boulders and cannonballs down upon the attackers. After hours of hand-to-hand combat, the Union troops solemnly withdrew. Sherman's offensive had been turned back.

During all of this action, the Washington Blues were held in reserve. They waited in the center of the line, and their officers paced back and forth nervously.

Sergeant Pickens examined the slope ahead of them with narrowed eyes. "I sure hope we don't have to go up that hill," he muttered to himself.

His words, however, reached Royal. He looked up to where the Confederate guns peered down. The muzzles had an evil look to them, and Royal shivered. "It'd be like sticking your head in a cannon to try to go up that hill!"

Ira shook his head. "I don't think they'll ask us to make a charge like that. Too many Confederates up there."

The squad kept looking upward to where General Bragg's headquarters were in full view. His officers were coming and going constantly.

As they watched, Sergeant Pickens said, "Look— they're bringin' in new troops. If we're gonna go, we better go before they get the place fully manned."

What the Union officers did not know was that General Bragg had divided his forces. He had sent some troops into rifle pits at the bottom of the ridge, while the rest were on the crest. He had also given orders that the men in the rifle pits, if attacked, were to fire one volley and then withdraw up the hill. Unfortunately, Bragg failed to tell the officers on top of the ridge of this order.

Suddenly bugles sounded. Drums began to rattle.

"There's the order to advance," Ira said. "Let's go."

Royal's mouth was dry, and he found it hard to breathe. It was always so for him when a battle started. But obeying orders, he started forward with the rest of the squad. Up and down the line he saw the Army of the Cumberland moving ahead. He saw also that the servants, the cooks, and the clerks had found guns somewhere and had joined the ranks.

"It looks like the cooks are tired of gettin' left out," Rosie said. "They're aimin' to make a fight out of it."

Drake felt nothing. This was strange, for previously he had either felt a great thrill at going into battle or awful fear that shook him badly. Now, however, as he strode forward, he again just felt like a man with a job to do—like a carpenter who had a box to build. There were certain boards to be sawed, certain nails to be driven, certain tasks to be done, and he somehow felt calm, almost as if he were an observer.

The drums continued to rattle, and to each side of him men ran forward over the rough, broken ground.

They all were under the command of General Thomas. This general had been so strict in drilling his men that the lines were ruler straight. The band played as the banners fluttered. When suddenly they emerged onto the plain at the foot of Missionary Ridge, twenty thousand strong, they must have made a fearsome sight for the Confederates watching from the mountaintop a mile away.

Then abruptly six rapid cannon blasts split the air—the signal to advance—and Drake moved forward with the great blue line.

Artillery began to thunder from both sides. Atop the ridge, the Confederates opened up and were answered by the Union guns below. Drake's ears were smitten by the immense roar as with a heavy blow.

He saw that the Rebel artillery was knocking huge holes in the blue line of which he was a part. He saw some men falter. One fell to the ground, not wounded but terrified. Drake glanced at him with compassion as the boy covered his head with his hands.

Ira Pickens prodded the soldier to his feet, but the young man was petrified. The sergeant left him and went on. He looked over at Drake. "You all right, Drake?" he called.

"Sure," Drake answered. His eyes were now on the rifle pits ahead.

Suddenly minié balls were whistling and zipping past his ears. He felt his hat shift and knew that a bullet had passed through it. In front of him a man went down, his face torn by a shell fragment. For Drake, now was the time for fear to surely come, but it did not. He walked on.

Then he heard Pickens shout, "They're running, boys! Let's take those rifle pits!"

Drake ran forward, aware that Royal was on his right and Rosie on his left.

"Watch out for them Rebels!" Rosie yelled. "They ain't give up yet."

"Watch yourself, Rosie!" Drake called back, and then they rushed at the barricade behind which the Confederates had hidden themselves.

"They're going up the hill!" Ira Pickens yelled.

Lieutenant Smith had been running up and down the blue line. His orders were to take the rifle pits, and he saw that his men, though suffering losses, had now achieved that objective.

But then something happened to the Army of the Cumberland. These troops had been looked down on during most of the war. They had no big victories to point to and had been tormented by other Yankee soldiers. But now they had a slight taste of victory. *They had taken the rifle pits!*

And suddenly that seemed not enough. There were shouts all up and down the line, and Lieutenant Smith was astonished to see his men rushing toward the mountain, yelling and screaming.

"Come back, you fools!" he shouted, but he might as well have been hollering at the trees for all the notice his men took.

Drake lunged forward too. "Come on," he said, "let's take that hill!"

"Wait a minute!" Rosie gasped, but when he saw men charging wildly upward, he grunted. "Well, I guess with my ailments, I might as well take a chance." He stumbled over the rough ground and soon was fighting the brambles and the saplings with the others.

141

Back at Grant's command post, the general wheeled furiously on General Thomas. "Thomas," he barked, "who ordered those men up the ridge?"

"I don't know," Thomas said. "*I* didn't."

Grant turned on General Granger. "Did you order them up, Granger?"

"No," said Granger, "they started without orders." Then with quiet satisfaction he said, "When those men get started, all the devils in the pit won't stop them."

General Grant turned his field glasses toward the mountain. He was watching a battle gone out of control—a general's nightmare!

He had never once considered a major assault by Thomas's troops. The attacking force was weaker than the Confederate force! Moreover, they were attacking Bragg's line at what he supposed was its strongest point. This unplanned attack could lead to total disaster.

Grant considered calling the men back, but then an officer heard him mutter, "It's all right—if it turns out all right." He added, "If not, somebody will suffer for this."

Neither Drake nor any of the other men scrambling up the side of Missionary Ridge could know what Grant was thinking. All they knew was that they were getting heavy fire from above.

Then something happened that was in their favor. The Confederates in the rifle pits left after firing their first volley. Those were their orders. But to the men on the ridge, it looked as if they were retreating. This sent panic into the troops at the top of the hill.

Also, the Rebels quickly discovered that they could not aim their cannon low enough to fire down the sheer mountainside. And the Union troops kept on crawling upward, only pausing from time to time to reload.

Bullets clipped the small trees that Drake used to haul himself along. A branch cut by a ball fell to the ground in front of him. But some sort of battle madness was upon him now. He had run before, but he would not run this time!

As he climbed, he remembered Lori's words: *You'll be a better soldier from now on.* There was some grim satisfaction to that, he thought, although he did not have time to think of it long.

The Confederates on the crest began to run. This was something the Army of Tennessee had never done in two and a half years of hard fighting. But the morale of the men was shaken by the wave of blue troops that swarmed upward in spite of all the Rebel firepower.

Shouts of triumph rang through the Union ranks, and Drake felt his heart beating hard. "We've got 'em!" he yelled.

But one group of Confederates was perched along the edge of a ravine in a V-shaped defensive position. And through this ravine Sgt. Ira Pickens rushed with his squad. Immediately the Rebels above began pouring a terrible fire down upon them. Seeing his men begin to drop, Pickens shouted, "Take cover! They got us pinned down!"

Along with the others, Drake threw himself behind a boulder. His blood beat in his ears as he pounded powder and ball into his musket.

For some fifteen minutes the battle raged in that little area. Pickens saw that his men were being cut to pieces. He stood and yelled, "We've got to get around that—" And he fell backward, struck by a minié ball.

In an instant Drake was by his side. "Are you all right, Sarge?"

"They got me in the side." Ira looked at him, his eyes wild. "Drake—you got to lead the men out of here. See . . . grove of oak trees? Take 'em through there . . . get out of . . . this place."

Drake saw that Ira was losing consciousness. He ripped open the sergeant's uniform, quickly formed a bandage of his handkerchief, and managed to fasten it over the wound. Then he shouted, "Hey, the sarge has been hit!"

From behind the rocks the squad looked toward him. Several men seemed to be wounded. At least three members appeared to be dead.

The fire from above increased, but Drake did not stop to think. He picked up the limp form of Sergeant Pickens and threw him over his shoulder. He thanked God for strength, hardly realizing that he had done so.

Bullets began to rain around him, but he yelled, "This way! Follow me!" He seemed to have been given supernatural strength, for he carried his musket in his right hand and held onto the semiconscious sergeant with his left. As he crossed the opening of the V-shaped valley, bullets kicked up branches and dust at his feet. Miraculously, he was not hit.

"Come on," he yelled again and plunged ahead. "This way!"

"Follow Bedford!" Royal shouted and leaped up from his hiding place.

The rest of the squad followed, dodging and ducking across the open space, until all were in the shelter of the trees.

Lieutenant Smith approached from the other direction. He had apparently seen the men being shot to pieces. Leaning over the wounded Pickens, he asked, "How are you, Sergeant?"

Ira opened his eyes and said more strongly than Drake would have thought he could, "I'm all right— got a little scratch, but we're out of there." He turned his eyes to Bedford and tried to grin. "If I had a medal to give, I'd give it to you, Drake. You sure saved our bacon that time!"

Lieutenant Smith turned to Drake. "I'll take care of the medal. You did a good job, Bedford. I'll see that the colonel hears about it." He glanced about him then. "We've got to take the rest of this hill. Rosie, you stay with the sergeant—get him back to the lines where that wound can be treated. The rest of you, come on. Bedford, you're acting sergeant."

Drake gaped at him in disbelief. "Not me, Lieutenant. Any one of these fellas—"

"The rest of these fellas didn't carry their sergeant out under fire and lead the rest of the squad. And don't worry—you probably won't be a sergeant any longer than it takes to fight this battle."

Drake found that amusing. "Well, all right—on that condition." He looked at the other men. "You fellas ready to go?"

Royal said, "Sure, Drake, you lead the way."

Drake exchanged a long glance with Royal Carter. He remembered their personal battle and how he had put this man on the ground. And now here was Royal, supporting him. He said, "You

145

ought to be doing this, Royal, but let's go up together."

The two of them led the way.

Behind them, Rosie said to Walter Beddows,
"That Drake Bedford, he's all kinds of a feller."

"He sure is," Beddows answered. "I thought he
was a dead man when he came charging out of
there with the sergeant on his shoulders. He ought
to get a medal for that for sure—or at least maybe
be made corporal."

"Me, I'd rather have some of my kidney medicine. I think I'm beginning to get complications."

15

A New Beginning

General Grant sent a telegram to Washington:

> Although the battle lasted from nearly dawn until dark this evening, I believe I am not premature in announcing a complete victory over Bragg. Lookout Mountain, all the rifle pits in Chattanooga Valley, and Missionary Ridge entirely have been carried, and are now held by us.

General Bragg's army had indeed been routed, though the Confederates managed to withdraw aboard trains and on foot. Rebel casualties for the three days totaled 6,700 soldiers killed or wounded or captured, higher than the losses of the Union— 5,800 men.

The South would never recover from the fighting around Chattanooga. The gateway to the heart of the Confederacy had been flung open, and General Sherman was already planning a Federal advance on the city of Atlanta.

"Looks like we'll all be generals if this keeps up. Look at them stripes!" Rosie was admiring the new stripes that had been given not to Drake Bedford but to Royal Carter.

Royal had expressed shock when Lieutenant Smith informed him that he would be promoted to

147

take Ira Pickens's place. "But I'm not the soldier Ira is!" he protested.

Lieutenant Smith said, "You'll do until he gets back. You got a good squad here, Sergeant Carter. Now let's see you pull 'em together until we get the Rebels penned up in Atlanta."

Royal's squad gathered around him, teasing him about his promotion.

"Well, Professor, I guess we'll have to call you Sergeant now." Walter Beddows punched him on the arm. "Hard to have respect for a fellow you grew up with, but like the lieutenant says, you'll do until the real sergeant gets back."

Drake Bedford grinned. There was a confidence and a jaunty air about him. He was his old self again. Drake had learned something since coming into the army. He had been humbled, and he now felt that he had been really accepted by his company.

"Now that you're the sergeant," Rosie was saying, "I been meaning to tell you—I think I better not be assigned any hard work for a few days. Not until I get my arthritis settled back some."

A laugh went up, and the teasing turned in Rosie's direction.

Drake thought about his own possible promotion. He had no desire to ever be a sergeant. "It's one thing," he explained to Rosie, "to do something that takes just a few minutes—like when we were under fire. But being a sergeant, you got to be regular and steady every day."

Later on in the week, General Thomas came by and reviewed the troops. Thomas was a huge, powerful man with a thick beard and penetrating eyes.

He stopped his horse in front of the Washington Blues and congratulated the major.

"Your men did a fine job, Major," he said. "I never saw soldiers behave any better under fire. I'll keep you in mind when we have hard jobs in the future."

"Oh, me!" Rosie mumbled. "There you are. Once you do a good thing, these generals expect you to keep it up."

Lieutenant Smith dismissed the company, then said to Royal, "Sergeant, I order you and Bedford to go with me into town and bring supplies out." Then a grin turned up the corners of his mouth. "And on the way back I think you'll have time to stop and see some old friends."

The old friends proved to be Mr. and Mrs. Jenkins. They pulled the two young soldiers inside, and Mr. Jenkins pounded their shoulders until they were ready to drop.

"You fellers are heroes!" he said. "If I was a drinking man, I'd pour out a toast, but I guess it'll have to be buttermilk."

"That suits me," Royal said. "I'd rather have buttermilk than wine anytime."

For a victory celebration, Mrs. Jenkins served hot biscuits and buttermilk with some fresh-ground sausage and newly laid eggs.

Lori sat between the boys at the table, listening as they told about the battle.

Royal said right away, "*I'll* tell all the stories." He stressed how Drake had saved his squad from being destroyed. "They didn't give him a medal either, but they should have," he concluded. He smirked at

Drake. "Now, don't say I haven't done my best to embellish your reputation, Private."

"Oh, I think that's wonderful!" Lori said, her eyes bright as she fixed them on Drake.

"He makes it sound like a lot more than it was," Drake protested.

"No, I don't," Royal disagreed. "You earned your keep up on that mountain. Everybody in the company admires you for it. And Major Bates came by and told Drake what a good soldier he was."

Drake felt very uncomfortable under all the praise. He was glad when the meal was over and they moved away from the table.

"You young folks go on outside. Show them that new calf we got, Lori," Mr. Jenkins said. "Ma and I'll do the dishes."

The three walked outdoors. Cold air blew over the mountains. The trees were orange and brown or were already stripped.

After they had admired the calf, Lori said, "Let's go down to the pond. I'll show you where I caught a big catfish last summer."

Dry leaves crunched under their feet as they made their way through an oak glade. Squirrels were active in the trees. Overhead a big red squirrel with a bushy tail chattered at them angrily as if they were invading his territory.

"I wish I had my musket," Drake remarked. "I'd have squirrel stew for supper."

"No, that's an old friend of mine," Lori protested. "He never fusses like that when I come by myself."

She led them down a twisting path under the huge oak branches. They came at last to a small creek that had been dammed up, making a pond some twenty feet across.

She pointed. "Right there's where I caught the biggest catfish you ever saw."

"Wonder if there are any more in there," Royal speculated. "If my sister Leah were here and that boyfriend of hers—Jeff Majors—they'd be fishing right now." He noticed a fallen log. "Let's sit on that log for a while. You can tell us more lies about how big that fish was, Lori."

They sat and talked. Overhead a flight of ducks made a V that scored the gray sky. Looking up, Royal said, "Goin' south."

Drake looked up at the birds too. "Like us. We'll be headed south pretty soon too."

"When?" Lori asked quickly.

"Nobody knows for sure, but we'll be going after the Rebels. And they'll go to Atlanta."

"And they'll fight every step of the way," Drake said. "I once thought they'd soon give up, but I don't think now they ever will."

A silence fell over the trio, then suddenly Drake turned to Royal. "I want to say something to you, Royal."

"Why, sure, Drake. What is it?"

Drake shifted his weight and said, "Back there in Pineville, when I forced that fight on you—well, I was wrong to do that."

"I've forgotten all about it."

"Well, maybe you have, but I haven't. Guess I'll have to ask you to forgive me for that."

Royal grinned broadly. "Why, sure, Drake. Don't think about it anymore."

Drake looked down at his boots, then up at Lori.

"And I guess," he said slowly, "I never went courtin' like this."

Startled, Lori said, "Why, what do you mean, Drake?"

"Well . . . always before, I tried to cut the other fellow out, get the girl all by herself. And now here we are, Royal and me, both in love with you, and here you are, right between us."

Lori's cheeks turned rosy. For once she seemed unable to think of anything to say. She lowered her head and clasped her hands.

Royal laughed aloud. "It *is* a strange kind of courting. You're not embarrassed, are you, Lori? Most girls would love to have two men chasing after them."

"Well, I don't like it," Lori said. "I mean," she added quickly, exchanging a glance first with Royal, then with Drake. "I think so much of both of you!"

"Well, both of us think so much of you." Drake saw that she was indeed deeply embarrassed. "Don't feel bad. It's not your fault that you got two fellows going out of their heads about you."

"It's not like that at all," she said. "You're just lonesome and away from home. You're not in love with me—neither one of you."

"You're wrong about that, Lori," Royal said, "but it's not fair to put you on the spot. Tell you what, Drake—I'll show that I'm the better man."

Royal reached over and took Lori's hand, and she looked at him in surprise. Shaking it firmly, he said, "Good-bye, Lori. I'll write to you from wherever we go. I hope you'll write back, and sooner or later I'll be seeing you." He got up and walked away, his feet crunching the leaves noisily.

Drake stared after him. "Well, that son of a gun! He *is* a better man than I am!"

"He's sweet, isn't he?"

"I don't know about calling my buddy *sweet,*" Drake said, "but not many fellows would do what he just did."

He waited until Royal disappeared. Then he said, "Lori, I never told you about what happened on Lookout Mountain. When it all started and the going got pretty bad, all I could remember was that you said that God had told you that I'd be a better soldier. And you were right. It must've been God."

"I'm so glad. You have so much to offer, Drake. You could do anything you wanted to."

"I'm not sure about that." He looked in the direction of the trees where Royal had disappeared. "But I'm gonna try and be as good a fellow as Royal Carter. I'm not going to romance you, much as I'd like to." He stood and pulled Lori to her feet. "I'll say the same thing that Royal said. I'm going to write you, and someday you'll look up and you'll see a fellow coming and you'll say, 'There's Drake Bedford. He's come a-courting.'"

"I wish you didn't have to go, Drake."

"But I do. Come—I want to catch up with Royal. We'll walk back to camp together."

They caught up with Royal before he reached the house.

"Don't walk so fast!" Drake said. "We've got to get all the way back to camp."

Royal looked at his friend and said, "All right, Drake. Let's walk together."

"Now," Lori said, "just a minute." She pulled Drake's head down and kissed him on the cheek. Then she turned to Royal and did the same thing.

"That's my good-bye for now. I'll write the both of you." Tears were in her eyes as she turned and walked quickly toward the house.

Drake looked at Royal. "One of us is goin' to get an awful jolt one of these days."

Royal nodded soberly, and then he smiled. "But one of us is going to get a mighty fine girl!"

16
A Surprise for Sarah

Sarah was sitting in front of the mirror, brushing her hair. The curtains were drawn back, and the yellow beams of sunlight threw bars on the figured carpet. They also highlighted her dark hair and played over the rose-colored robe that she wore. As she drew the comb down through her lustrous raven locks, she leaned forward and examined her face.

On her right cheek was one small scar, so tiny as to be almost unnoticeable. This, along with two others on the left side of her forehead at the hairline, were all that remained of the dread smallpox.

Sarah took a deep breath and offered up a brief prayer of thanksgiving. "Thank You, Jesus, for healing me," she said, her dark eyes looking back at her from the mirror. She realized how fortunate she had been. Some others who had been struck down had been scarred badly.

A knock came at her door, and she looked up eagerly. "Come in!"

A cheerful Leah entered, carrying a tray. "I brought up your lunch. And I see you're primping and admiring yourself. You must be getting well."

"Don't be awful, Leah!" Sarah put down the brush and stood. For a moment the room seemed to sway, and she felt weak. The long-drawn-out illness had drained her strength.

"Be careful," Leah cried. "You're not strong yet. Here—sit down."

155

"I'm able to go down to the table," Sarah protested. Nevertheless, she took a seat and began to eat the food that Leah had put before her—a bowl of hot beef stew and fresh-made biscuits along with some canned tomatoes, which she loved.

Leah sat on the bed and watched her sister eat. There was a happy expression in her eyes. "You're looking so much better, and you're getting stronger every day."

"I feel better." Sarah took another spoonful of stew, then said, "Have you seen Tom this morning?"

"No, he and Ezra were around earlier, but I don't know where they got off to."

A frown marred the smoothness of Sarah's forehead, "He's been acting rather . . . well . . . strange lately, don't you think?"

"Strange? How do you mean, strange?"

"I mean, when I was real sick, he came every day, and he would sit beside me for hours. But for the last week he just pops in, asks me how I am, stays a few minutes, then he's gone. I wonder if he's upset with me."

"Oh, I don't think so. He hasn't said anything to me."

Sarah was perplexed. Tom's behavior was odd indeed. Since the time he had told her that he loved her and that he had a surprise for her, she had tried to pry out of him what the surprise was. Tom, however, had been adamant, offering nothing more than a grin and a promise—"Just wait and see. You're going to like it. I can tell you that much."

Sarah finished the stew and the tomatoes and began to sip her glass of tea. "What's the war news? Have you heard anything about the fighting?"

"Well, yes. I forgot to tell you. The paper came. There's been a great Union victory at Missionary Ridge, just outside Chattanooga."

Sarah looked up quickly and set down the tea. "I wonder if Royal was in that?"

Leah grew sober. "I think he must've been. It was an awful battle. The Union won, but the paper said there were a lot of losses." She hesitated. "The casualty list hasn't come out yet."

Sarah bit her lower lip, and her eyes were troubled. "I hate those casualty lists. Every time they read them down in the town square, you can hear a scream when some name is called. Some mother, or wife, or sister crying out. It's just awful."

"I know." Leah nodded sympathetically. "I wish they wouldn't do it like that. Now they've started to print the names in the newspaper."

At first the casualty lists were sent to various towns to be read aloud. Lately, however, it had been deemed kinder simply to print the lists and to let people look over them in private. Then, if the name of a loved one was included, they wouldn't make a public display of their grief.

"Have you heard from Jeff?" Sarah asked.

"Oh, yes." Leah sniffed and said, "He went to a party again with that Lucy Driscoll."

Sarah glanced at her sister. "You're jealous, aren't you?"

"Me? Jealous of that—that fluff!"

"Well, you told me she was very pretty."

"Jeff said I'm prettier than she is."

"You didn't let me read that part of your letter." Sarah smiled. "Go get it—I'd like to see it."

"No, I won't, but he said it all right; and he said other things too, but I won't tell you."

"That's all right. I don't think you should." Sarah smiled again. "I can't keep up with you. I still think of you and Jeff as little children out robbing birds' nests and catching perch out of the creek. Hard to believe that you both are growing up so fast. Why, I believe you are taller than I am now."

Sarah knew Leah was sensitive about her height, feeling herself to be too tall.

"I'm such a giant," Leah complained. "If I don't quit growing, I'll be taller than Jeff."

"No, you won't. Look how tall his father is—and Tom. Why, they're both over six feet."

"I will be too if I don't stop growing!"

"No, you won't. We don't have any six-foot women in our family. You just look nice and state-ly—like a queen. When you're not acting like a spoiled child, that is." And then Sarah said, "I wonder what Tom is doing with himself."

"Well, he's helping a lot more with the farm work now. He gets around real good. He milks the cows. I'm glad to get out of that job. Never did like milking."

"I just wish he'd come to see me. I'm going down to supper tonight. I don't care what Ma or anybody else says."

"Pa will take the switch to you if you don't mind."

Dan Carter was home from his trip as a sutler and had been happy to find Sarah on the mend.

"Though I think," Leah said cautiously, "you might come down to supper if you'll be very careful and let me help you."

"I'll do anything to get out of this room."

Sarah spent the afternoon impatiently waiting for suppertime, and when Leah finally came in a little before five, she exclaimed, "Let's go, Leah! Help me down those stairs!"

Sarah held onto her sister as the two navigated the steps, and when they entered the dining room she was startled by a burst of applause. She saw her father and mother standing on one side of the table, and Morena on the other side beside Tom. Ezra completed the group.

Sarah flushed. "All this fuss over supper?"

Dan Carter shook his head. "No, it's not that, Daughter. We're thankful to the Lord for sparing our family—especially you." He came around and kissed her before she sat down, something unusual for him.

When all were seated, her father did another unexpected thing. He said, "Tom, I'm going to ask you if you'll return thanks."

Sarah thought Tom looked a little surprised, but he bowed his head and said a simple prayer, thanking God for the food. He asked blessings on the Carter home, then said, "And be with my own family in Virginia."

A hearty "Amen" went up, and then they began to eat. Morena sat as close as she could to Ezra, for she had a special affection for the young hired hand. He fed her from his plate from time to time, and she would laugh happily.

The baby was perched in the high chair that Ezra had made. She took great pleasure in squashing the mashed potatoes and then licking them off her fingers.

"That would be disgusting if anybody else did it," Tom observed. "With Esther it's just cute." He considered her for a moment. "She's sure going to look like Ma. Same blonde hair and blue eyes."

"She's got the same features exactly," Mrs. Carter agreed. "Your mother was such a beautiful woman."

"I wish Pa could see Esther." Tom sighed. Then he perked up and looked over at Sarah. "Did you hear about the victory celebration, Sarah?"

"No," Sarah said. "For the victory at Lookout Mountain?"

"Sure. It's going to be next Saturday at the community hall." Tom cocked his head to one side and looked solemn. "As your physician, I'd say that you'll be just about ready, by that time, to get out of the house."

"Oh, I couldn't go, Tom!"

"Your doctor says you can, so get yourself ready. We're all going."

"That's a good idea," Ezra put in. "We ought to show our support for the army." Then he glanced at Tom. "I'm sorry, Tom—it can't be a 'victory celebration' for you. That's got to be hard."

Tom looked about the table. "As you know, the war's been over for me since Gettysburg," he said and paused. "I guess I might as well tell you—I've given up on the South winning. I think Pa has too—and Jeff, from what I hear. Oh, the fighting will go on for a while, but there's no way the South will win. So we'll just go to your victory celebration Saturday, and that will be it."

Tom Majors had thrown himself into the Confederate cause with all his heart, and it hurt Sarah terribly to see his world come crashing down.

Mr. Carter said quietly, "I wish everyone could look at it like that."

A murmur went around the table, and peace seemed to descend in an unusual way. Tom looked about at their faces. "One day," he said, "it'll all be

160

over." Then he broke the spell by saying sternly, "And you be ready Saturday, Miss Sarah Carter. Put your best party dress on. We'll let 'em see a retired Rebel and his lady friend."

Sarah stared back at him—the old Tom that she remembered so well. She smiled. "I'll be ready."

On the victory celebration day, Sarah was surprised when her mother presented her with a new party dress. It was pale green with dark green trim; and, despite her weight loss from her illness, it fit her well. She had slipped it on and was brushing her hair when Leah passed her bedroom door.

"It's time to go, Sarah."

"I'll be right there."

Sarah finished her hair, took one last look at herself, and touched the simple pearl earrings that she wore, a gift from her parents.

She was feeling much stronger now, able to go down the stairs without help.

She found the rest of the family waiting in the parlor.

Leah was putting a coat on Esther, who was protesting loudly. Ignoring the wails, Leah fastened the coat and then picked her up. "There, now you'll be nice and warm."

Ezra came in, wearing a new suit—a dark gray suit with a new, shiny white shirt and a black string tie.

"Why, you look downright handsome, Ezra!" Sarah said.

Ezra beamed. "Thank you, Sarah, and you look right pretty yourself. That's a new dress, isn't it?"

"Yes, do you like it?" Sarah turned around and

accepted everyone's compliments. Then her brow wrinkled. "So are we ready to go?"

"Just about," Ezra said, a mischievous look on his face. "I'll go get Tom."

As they stood waiting, Sarah said, "Your dress looks real nice too, Ma."

"I'm glad you like it. It's just an old one I made over, you know."

Silence fell over the room. Sarah was perplexed, for there seemed to be a strange feeling of—expectation?—among the occupants. Morena came over and felt her dress, and she took the girl's hand and patted her blonde hair. "You look real nice, sweetheart," she said. She herself had made Morena's dress. It was a cranberry color, and Morena looked like a doll.

Ezra came back. "Well, I guess we're all ready to go," he said, but he crossed the room to stand beside Leah, then faced the door.

Sarah looked toward the hallway, expecting Tom. But something was wrong. She realized suddenly that she was waiting for the tapping of his crutches on the floor. She did not hear them, however, so was startled when Tom, wearing a new light blue suit, appeared in the doorway.

And then she gasped. "Tom," she whispered, her eyes turning wide. "Tom, what—"

Tom walked across the room toward her, and there was a joyous light in his dark eyes. His walk was a little awkward, but nevertheless he was walking without the crutch.

Sarah looked downward and saw, instead of a pinned-up trouser leg, a shiny black boot! The left boot just like the right one!

"Oh, Tom!" She threw her arms around him. "I'm so happy."

"Well, I'm glad I've found a way to get a hug out of you!" Tom winked over her shoulder at Sarah's parents. Then he reached down and tapped the left boot. It made a wooden sound. "What do you think about your hired hand, Ezra, now? Ezra and I been working on this for a week."

"How's it feel, Tom?" Ezra asked.

"Feels fine, Ezra. You did a great job." Tom turned to explain to Sarah. "Ezra went all the way into Lexington to where they make things like this. He took along the measurements and the cast he'd made, and when he came back we had to practice with it."

Tom walked across the room. He spun around and said, "Look! How about that?"

"It's wonderful!" Sarah's eyes were like diamonds. Then there were tears in them. "Thank you, Ezra," she said. Then she turned back to Tom and held out her hands. "This *will* be a victory celebration, Tom. For you!"

It was a victory celebration indeed, for everyone in Pineville had been alerted that young Tom Majors had recovered in more ways than one. The news that he would no longer serve in the Confederate army, but would remain at Pineville for the duration of the war, had gone through the whole community.

Some had scoffed, saying, "You can't convert a Confederate Rebel." But after people talked with Tom and saw his earnestness, most accepted him. After all, he had grown up in this town. He and his family had been well liked and respected. And also it had become a mark of decency to take a young man at his word.

The high moment of the night for Sarah came when Tom said, "Well, I guess it's time to try this leg out for sure. You remember this song they're playing?"

Sarah remembered. It had been played at the last party they attended together.

The fiddler was grinning and nodding at him as if to say, "It's your turn, Tom."

"So may I have this dance?"

Sarah caught her breath. She had not thought Tom quite so daring, but she whispered, "Yes."

The music was slow, and Tom was steady on his feet. He smiled down at her. "Everybody's watching."

"And I know what they're seeing," Sarah whispered. "One of the bravest men I've ever known."

"No, they're seeing one of the prettiest girls in the world."

When the fiddling stopped, there was a wild burst of applause.

Tom held up his hands. "Thank you very much. It pleases me to see that things can be restored." The room grew very still as he added, "My father and my brother, Jeff, and I—we all love this place and think of it as home." He paused. "I'm looking forward to the day when the fighting is over and we can all be one people again. I'm grateful that God spared my life, and I'm thankful for people like you who are willing to forgive."

A muted "Amen" ran through the crowd, and Tom whispered, "Come on, Sarah, let's go outside before I start blubbering."

He closed the door behind them, and they walked slowly to the edge of the porch. Far off, the mountains were highlighted by moonlight, their tops turned to silver.

Quietness lay over the outside world. Inside, the music began again.

After several minutes of silence, Tom said, "You're still my girl, aren't you?"

"I always have been, Tom, and I always will be. And one day soon, I'll be Sarah Majors."

"It's what I've wanted for a long time. And I thank God for bringing us to this place."

The music played on. At the hitching rail, the horses chomped on the short, dead grass. Sarah and Tom turned and went back inside.

Get swept away in the many Gilbert Morris Adventures available from Moody Press:

"Too Smart" Jones

4025-8 Pool Party Thief
4026-6 Buried Jewels
4027-4 Disappearing Dogs
4028-2 Dangerous Woman
4029-0 Stranger in the Cave
4030-4 Cat's Secret
4031-2 Stolen Bicycle
4032-0 Wilderness Mystery
4033-9 Spooky Mansion
4034-7 Mysterious Artist

Come along for the adventures and mysteries Juliet "Too Smart" Jones always manages to find. She and her other homeschool friends solve these great adventures and learn biblical truths along the way. Ages 9-14

Seven Sleepers - The Lost Chronicles

3667-6 The Spell of the Crystal Chair
3668-4 The Savage Game of Lord Zarak
3669-2 The Strange Creatures of Dr. Korbo
3670-6 City of the Cyborgs
3671-4 The Temptations of Pleasure Island
3672-2 Victims of Nimbo
3673-0 The Terrible Beast of Zor

More exciting adventures from the Seven Sleepers. As these exciting young people attempt to faithfully follow Goel, they learn important moral and spiritual lessons. Come along with them as they encounter danger, intrigue, and mystery.
Ages 10-14

Dixie Morris Animal Adventures

3363-4 Dixie and Jumbo
3364-2 Dixie and Stripes
3365-0 Dixie and Dolly
3366-9 Dixie and Sandy
3367-7 Dixie and Ivan
3368-5 Dixie and Bandit
3369-3 Dixie and Champ
3370-7 Dixie and Perry
3371-5 Dixie and Blizzard
3382-3 Dixie and Flash

Follow the exciting adventures of this animal lover as she learns more of God and His character through her many adventures underneath the Big Top. Ages 9-14

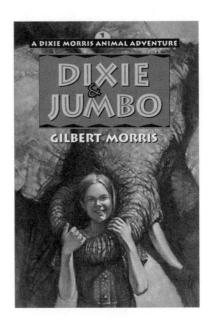

The Daystar Voyages

4102-X Secret of the Planet Makon
4106-8 Wizards of the Galaxy
4107-6 Escape From the Red Comet
4108-4 Dark Spell Over Morlandria
4109-2 Revenge of the Space Pirates
4110-6 Invasion of the Killer Locusts
4111-4 Dangers of the Rainbow Nebula
4112-2 The Frozen Space Pilot
4113-0 White Dragon of Sharnu
4114-9 Attack of the Denebian Starship

Join the crew of the Daystar as they traverse the wide expanse of space. Adventure and danger abound, but they learn time and again that God is truly the Master of the Universe. Ages 10-14

MOODY
The Name You Can Trust
1-800-678-8812   www.MoodyPress.org

Seven Sleepers Series

3681-1 Flight of the Eagles
3682-X The Gates of Neptune
3683-3 The Swords of Camelot
3684-6 The Caves That Time Forgot
3685-4 Winged Riders of the Desert
3686-2 Empress of the Underworld
3687-0 Voyage of the Dolphin
3691-9 Attack of the Amazons
3692-7 Escape with the Dream Maker
3693-5 The Final Kingdom

Go with Josh and his friends as they are sent by Goel, their spiritual leader, on dangerous and challenging voyages to conquer the forces of darkness in the new world. Ages 10-14

Bonnets and Bugles Series

0911-3 Drummer Boy at Bull Run
0912-1 Yankee Bells in Dixie
0913-X The Secret of Richmond Manor
0914-8 The Soldier Boy's Discovery
0915-6 Blockade Runner
0916-4 The Gallant Boys of Gettysburg
0917-2 The Battle of Lookout Mountain
0918-0 Encounter at Cold Harbor
0919-9 Fire Over Atlanta
0920-2 Bring the Boys Home

Follow good friends Leah Carter and Jeff Majors as they experience danger, intrigue, compassion, and love in these civil war adventures. Ages 10-14

MOODY
The Name You Can Trust
1-800-678-8812 www.MoodyPress.org